GIRL FACTORY

GIRL FACTORY

Jim Krusoe

Tin House Books

Published by Tin House Books, Portland, Oregon, and New York, New York Distributed to the trade by Publishers Group West, 1700 Fourth St., Berkeley, CA 94710, www.pgw.com

Library of Congress Cataloging-in-Publication Data

Krusoe, James.
 Girl factory / by Jim Krusoe. -- 1st U.S. ed.
    p. cm.
 ISBN 978-0-9794198-2-9
 I. Title.
 PS3561.R873G57 2008
 813'.54--dc22   2008001132

First U.S. edition 2008

Printed in Canada

ISBN 10: 0-9794198-2-4

Interior design by Laura Shaw Design, Inc.

www.tinhouse.com

e
RUSOE

FOR LEE

As a hero in everyday life I am a public menace.

—Peter Handke, *My Year in the No-Man's-Bay*

1

It was early on a Saturday morning. I'd been sitting in my kitchen, drinking coffee (black, two sugars), when I decided to carry the newspaper out to the balcony of my one-bedroom apartment and read it there. It was the sort of thing I liked to do when I had the time. I had just finished the comics, the weather report, and sports pages, and was deep into a section entitled Out and About when I came across the headline "Dog Too Smart for Own Good." But instead of the pleasant human-interest story I anticipated, I found a tale both darker and more disturbing.

According to the article, a dog named Buck, a particular mix of German shepherd, rottweiler, pit bull, and chow, was the product of a government-sponsored enterprise to create an animal of exceptional intelligence for use in the military. The whole course of the experiment had taken several generations of dogs to completely develop, the article explained. It added that, to the researchers' surprise, in the end they discovered that the gene for intelligence, at least in dogs, is somehow connected to the one for aggression.

It wasn't exactly that Buck was a mean dog, the reporter noted. Buck was far too intelligent for that. However, the animal's surly way and judgmental demeanor made many of those who worked with him feel so uncomfortable that they were unable to perform their own duties properly. They became self-conscious and began to make mistakes when the dog was around. The article hinted that there was more, but didn't say what. As a result, the army had released Buck to civilian life, but even there apparently he had a way about him that made people feel insecure. The unhappy result was that Buck was scheduled to be put down, and the entire breeding project had been written off as a failure. The newspaper named the location where Buck was being held prior to his execution. It was an animal shelter not far from where I lived.

I lowered the paper, picked up my cup of French roast, and looked out at the neighborhood. Below me and to my right, Captain Bloxheim in his plaid bathrobe was intent on watching his hose spray water onto a square of brownish grass. The loveable captain was a neighbor across the way, and had once been in charge of a cargo vessel in the Pacific. On second thought, he wasn't especially loveable, though he was still fit, and wore the kind of thin moustache that movie actors used to sport. From time to time he'd give me a piece of well-meaning advice, and I would nod to show I'd heard it. We were close and not, in the way that neighbors in an apartment complex often are. To my left, a small child was smashing a former table leg into splinters. Between them an old lady slowly made her way down the sidewalk. She listed badly to the right, her three-pronged aluminum cane thumping beside her like a claw.

Well, Jonathan, I thought, there they are, your fellow countrymen, all products of some random, flawed combination of genes that, good or bad, thanks to the Constitution of the United States of America, are being allowed to play themselves out in perfect freedom on the highways and byways of our cities and states as best they can. And meanwhile a helpless animal, an innocent by-product of man's tampering with the sacred code of nature, will not be allowed even a chance. It didn't seem fair.

Certainly, I reasoned, Buck hadn't asked to be created only to have his life snatched away just because some overly fastidious bureaucrat had changed his mind any more than the three humans beneath my balcony, or me, for that matter—I hadn't exactly chosen my fate. Not for the first time, I was sickened by the arrogance of my own species, by the arrogance of all humans, by mankind's endless capacity for cruelty, artificial limitations, and prisons.

St. Nils's only animal shelter was about halfway between my apartment and my job at Mister Twisty's yogurt parlor, and for the most part I didn't give it much thought. I walked by it on the way to work about ten most mornings, and then in the evenings or late at night passed it again on the way back home, but at that moment, reading the paper, I was suddenly struck by how, hypocrite that I was, each time I passed the shelter I picked up my pace ever so slightly in order to leave behind the smell of urine and feces and the primal stink of animal fear. That Saturday, however, that very morning, was my chance to make amends and face things head-on. I'd been given the day off from Mister Twisty's so that my boss, Spinner, could repair the refrigeration equipment, and while he did, the entire place would be closed. Just suppose, I thought, I pay Buck a little visit, if only to see for myself exactly what the situation is, and maybe to let Buck know that all humans aren't as bad as those cold-blooded researchers—that some of us are deeply ashamed of the acts of our fellow men. Some of us, possibly a great many of us in fact, want only to apologize from the very bottom of our stunted and selfish human hearts.

It was still chilly out, so I went back inside to find a jacket, and it was really more as an afterthought than anything that I took along a crowbar, slipping it up my sleeve so as not to alarm anyone.

Keeping one arm straight at my side in as natural a fashion as possible, I soon arrived at the shelter and asked the person at the front desk ("Animal Technician One" was stenciled on her shirt) where the dogs waiting for adoption were kept. Without even looking up from a game of solitaire on her computer screen, she pointed wearily to my left, to a set of double doors from which a continuous stream of barks, howls, and yelps emanated. "Jesus, send this idiot on his way *tout de suite*," her gesture seemed to imply. I noted with some satisfaction that she appeared to be losing her stupid card game. I wasn't big on games, except for chess.

I walked through the doors into a large area intersected by a maze of chain-link fencing. Not wanting to arouse suspicion, I strolled between the rows of cages as if I were looking for a pet, but really keeping an eye out for where the shelter might have stashed its most famous boarder, Buck. I wasn't so naïve as to believe that in the aftermath of the article in the paper some supervisor would not have understood the need for security precautions, however minimal. Still, as disinterested as I was pretending to be, the sight that spread before me was enough to break a person's heart: the litters of fat-bellied pups playing, napping, leaping up to greet visitors in the very shadow of the cast-iron gas chamber beyond the corridors of cages; the lean old dogs, somehow sensing the impossibility of adoption, lifting their eyes like the inhabitants of a terminal nursing home to each visitor who walked by the doors of their pens, hoarding their energy for a last-ditch tail wag or two, not even staggering up from the cold concrete floors where they lay in the sun, hopelessly trying to warm themselves one last time before the final chill; the plain-looking dogs, brown or black, or brown and black, furiously yapping for someone to take them home, as if against all odds they might somehow distinguish themselves from every other plain-looking dog yapping for exactly the same thing; and then, saddest of all in their way, the snarlers and the growlers, the exact fierceness they had worked so hard to cultivate and which they now displayed so bravely being the very trait that would seal them to their fates, their pathetic biographies on display for all to see—the families moved away, the divorces, the stories of having bitten some child who'd spent an entire morning (when he or she should have been in school) prodding the poor animal with a stick until the kid finally ran home with a couple of deep scratches on his face or a few puncture wounds in her arm and the very first thing the avaricious parents did was get on the phone with their lawyer and threaten to sue the dog's miserable owners, themselves the helpless flotsam of the human race.

Still, I thought, these dogs *had* kept the faith; *they* were the ones who had waited in the heat tied to tubular metal bicycle racks outside supermarkets; *they* were the ones who had to go outside to crap on days too cold or wet or too anything, when their owners even bothered to get up off the couch to open the door; *they* were the ones who had stood by their blue or red or green food bowls patiently drooling for a refill of essentially inedible processed mush; *they* had lain quiet and full of hope near thresholds, holding heavy, bad-tasting brown leashes in their mouths, had panted in overheated cars, had shivered in the rain to be let in, had waited alone in the dark for hours in empty, badly decorated apartments while their owners were busy screwing out their pathetic brains in hopeless one-night stands at somebody else's bachelor or bachelorette pad.

And what had been their reward for all of this? Only to be tossed off at the first sign of inconvenience, at the first pressed-wood Ikea sofa leg chewed just a little out of boredom, at the first peed-on imitation Persian rug, at the first alcoholic neighbor to complain that their barking interrupted his or her alleged concentration, at the first uprooted *begonia plant*, for goodness' sake. There they were, these dogs, with their once so pleasantly pretentious names: Duke, and Prince, and Major, curled now in damp and stinking corners or sitting at the doors of their kennels staring out, hopelessly waiting for the faces of their loved ones, none of whom would ever, ever appear again—all these faithful dogs, these trusting companions, all these poor doomed innocents, waiting for the gas.

But where among these unfortunates was Buck? I had walked up and down row after row of cages when at last I noticed a barrier of yellow tape across one corridor. It read CAUTION, like the kind of warnings that workers put up at accidents and gas leaks, and so I approached the sagging barrier and looked cautiously beyond it. There, down a long row of empty, open cages, I spotted one that had been closed with a heavy lock. I peered around and, seeing no one, ducked under the tape to discover for myself what sort of a beast was being kept under such tight security.

What I found was a largish dog with short brown hair, a dark, square muzzle, and black-rimmed ears that stood as straight as sentinels, one on each side of a broad, intelligent-looking skull. His eyes were deep-set and brown, and when he looked at me I felt myself blush at my own unentitled presumption, almost as if I'd been caught staring at a young mother playing with her child, perhaps on a blanket in the shade of a pleasant tree in a park, when she had thought they were alone.

The animal lifted his gaze to examine me for an unusually long moment, and then, shaking his head slightly from side to side, apparently decided that I was of no consequence. As he resumed pawing at some wood chips on the floor of his cage, I took a step back to indicate my respect for his privacy but continued to observe him. Every so often he would move a piece of wood, then stare, then move it elsewhere. Something was going on, but I couldn't figure out what, until I noticed that some of the pieces were relatively dark and others lighter. And then I understood: unless I was terribly mistaken, this magnificent animal was replaying Boris Spassky's losing game against Anatoly Karpov during the 1973 Soviet Chess Championship in Moscow. My eyes opened wider, and I could feel the space inside my brain swell with admiration for any creature who, like Socrates himself, could remain so calm and so disinterested on the very eve of his execution.

From time to time the dog glanced up, probably curious as to what I was doing there and also, I thought, just possibly amused to find himself the object of such empathetic scrutiny by the first human he had ever met who was capable of taking the full measure of his intelligence. If he was aggressive, he wasn't showing it, except for a certain recklessness in the way he moved his knights. I was no chess expert, but it looked very much as if he had found a solution too late for the disappointed Boris.

Whether or not this was true I was never to learn, however, because I was interrupted by a noise back by the yellow tape. When I turned I saw a skinny man in a khaki shirt and matching pants observing me. "Hey you," he said, "get the hell out of there."

I could, of course, simply have smiled, walked over to the uniformed stranger, apologized, and left the proud dog to his fate; but emboldened by the admirable canine's own coolheadedness (and also curious about whether he *would* pull off the win for Spassky), I decided to ignore this particular functionary. This decision, wise or not, seemed to outrage the man.

He yelled again and grabbed one of those shovel/dustpan contraptions they kept around the place to clean up. Then he banged it smartly on the ground as if to get my attention. "Hey you," he repeated. "You asshole."

For the first time the dog paused his chess game and watched me with genuine interest. "Buck," I said, "don't worry. This isn't your fight; it's mine, Big Fellow."

The animal rose to all four of his massive feet and pressed his muzzle against the door of the cage. "The lock," he seemed to be telling me. "Whatever you do, don't forget the lock."

The man came toward me, and I cannot say the reason exactly—the low pay, the completely tasteless uniforms, or even the constant sight of all those animals they cannot save—but I have often observed, both before and since that day, that people who work in such places, though I am perfectly willing to believe they may start out with the best intentions, soon (very soon, in fact) become hardened, rigid, even authoritarian.

Suddenly at my side, the man grabbed a sleeve of my jacket and began to tug as if he'd convinced himself that I was merely a visitor from another land who, not understanding English, needed only a more forceful and physical sort of demonstration.

"Stop," I said, and gave him a slight shove to remind him that he should keep his distance.

But it was this very gesture more than anything else that seemed to infuriate him. He lifted the scooping thing he had brought with him and began to wave it in the air, as if he were going to launch an attack from the sky. And then all at once he did: as swift as an eagle the scoop plunged down, narrowly missing my shoulder. Fearful for my safety, I whipped out the crowbar (which I'd almost forgotten about) and motioned that he should stay away. Incredibly, he still chose to ignore me, and when he raised his ludicrous weapon a second time, I was forced to give him a tap across his forehead, rather harder than I'd intended, I'm afraid, at which point he slumped in total silence to the ground, his legs twitching just a little.

Once I had been goaded to a course of action, I had no choice but to continue. Taking the bloody crowbar, I pried open the door of the dog's cage—the lock was strong, but the door itself, with the usual municipal logic to save money, had been made of a flimsy alloy—and popped it open.

"Freedom, Buck," I said. "You've got your freedom, guy."

The dog looked at me for a moment, as if to assess his new-found situation and my role in it. Then, with a tremendous leap forward, he raced straight down the corridor into a group of Cub Scouts, seized a smallish boy by his neck, and began to shake him hard. When the boy stopped moving, the dog flipped the Scout's blue-clad body over his mighty shoulder and headed for the exit, only to be met there by an old woman who, possibly confused by the sight of such a large animal carrying a uniformed child, made the mistake of blocking his path and shouting, "Stop!" and "Help!" Flinging the limp Scout to the ground, the now-freed dog turned his attention to the old lady, crushing the top of her head with a sound that was not at all the sound I would have predicted—which would have been that of an egg being cracked—but more of a pop, the noise of a paper cup compressed against the ground by a heavy heel. And it was that very noise, the pop, like an old-fashioned flashbulb on a camera, which seemed to freeze the whole scene into the finished photograph that would later be pasted into the album of my memory. There I was, still holding my crowbar, standing in one corner above the no-longer-twitching-or-troublemaking kennel attendant, while in the other corner of the picture's frame the dog was looking up from the old lady, perhaps as startled as I was at what was taking place, and in the center were all the people who had come early that morning, presumably to choose a puppy or bring home a darling kitten, their mouths now agape, their eyes now wide open, their fingers now pointed accusingly in my direction, and also, I suppose, a good percentage of them now reconsidering their decisions to adopt.

The dog was the first to unfreeze from the photo. Once back in action, he left the old lady where she lay, picked up the Cub Scout again, and bolted through the gates.

And as for me, I was the very next to unfreeze.

Spotting a low wall in the rear of the shelter near the animal-disposal unit, I leapt over it, and, finding myself in an alley, turned left and ran for my life. It must have been the correct choice, because by the time my pursuers arrived I was gone, and they, having turned right instead, never even got close. At least that's what I guess happened.

At the time, of course, I had no idea how things would work out, or even if I *had* lost my pursuers, so I just kept moving and, like a lost dog, ran and dodged around corners and sprinted straight ahead until, finally, when I had put enough miles between me and the scene of the animal's crime, I sat down on a bench and began to think about my future. I was tired and hungry and hot, and I hadn't taken any extra cash with me that morning. Why should I have? Who could have anticipated the day's events? What could I do next? I couldn't take a cab or a bus, and even though I could hitchhike somewhere, the police were probably at that very minute watching the roads out of town. There was only one thing to do: I returned to my apartment to take my chances, to wait for a knock on the door, to hear the muffled words "Open up; it's the police," followed by the jangle of handcuffs and the roar of a squad car's engine.

At home that evening, I made a can of mushroom soup and a toasted cheese sandwich. I hadn't eaten since the morning, and they tasted good. I made another sandwich and watched the news, which was when I heard the sweetest words of all: *perpetrator unknown.*

I got up and made another sandwich, with roasted eggplant this time. I'd heard of nervous eating, of course, but I supposed that if ever there had been a time for me to come down with that particular disorder, this was it. I carried the sandwich into my bedroom, where I looked at the poster above my dresser. It depicted dozens of animals that were extinct, or were about to be. It seemed to say, "Welcome to the club, Jonathan."

I walked back to the kitchen and ate a pickle, and after that, because all that salt had made me thirsty, two glasses of iced tea without sugar. Finally I returned to the bedroom, where I lay on the bed, my eyes wide open, my ears straining to hear the sound of patrol cars gliding quietly to surround my building, and for the clunk of SWAT team armor, until it grew late, very late in the night.

At some point I guess I must have fallen asleep.

2

When I woke I was still a free man.

I ate my breakfast—a three-egg omelet with cream cheese and onions—and considered never leaving my apartment again or, alternatively, taking a bus out of town. That would be exactly the sort of thing the authorities would expect, however, and if I didn't show up at Mister Twisty's, Spinner just might worry enough to call the police, who, I was sure, wouldn't take long to add two and two. I hadn't been working at Mister Twisty's all that long, three or four months, after a series of unsatisfactory jobs: bicycle messenger, busboy, sales consultant, and housepainter's assistant. In comparison, employment at Mister Twisty's was practically a vacation, and it came with all the yogurt I could eat.

I dressed and left for work, attempting a normal-seeming wave to Captain Bloxheim, who was already up, holding out his hose to water the ivy. Needless to say, I wasn't so foolish as to walk by the animal shelter. I gave it a wide berth, and the result was that, for the first time ever, I was going to be late for work.

So I walked as quickly as I could until, in the distance, perched on one of the buildings in an ordinary-looking corner shopping mall, I spotted the familiar gigantic statue, an apparition in white and blue strapped to the roof with a sign below that read, "A Tasty Treat That's Good to Eat," followed by the words "Mister Twisty's Yogurt."

"You're late," Spinner said to me.

My boss was a tall, narrow individual in his early fifties with an unusually large Adam's apple. That morning I noticed a patch of hair on his cheek that he must have missed shaving for several days in a row, but this was no time to point it out. His hands were large, his fingers hirsute but clean, with short, thick nails. His posture was poor, possibly from leaning over a counter serving cups of yogurt day in and day out. Though I had passed my probationary period, we were not exactly pals.

"Yes," I answered. "I had a bad night trying to sleep, and when I finally did shut my eyes I couldn't wake in time. I'm sorry."

Spinner gave me a funny look. "OK," he said, "see that it doesn't happen again. The yogurt business is not for sissies, Jonathan, but if you treat it well it will treat you well in turn."

"Thanks," I said, and I meant it; I would have hated to lose this job. After that I went about my usual routine. I swept the floor, refilled the napkin dispensers, and checked the swirl machines to see that they were working properly. Every time the front door opened I held my breath. Every time a customer I didn't recognize sat down at the counter I was afraid it would be some tenderhearted individual who had been out adopting a dog the day before. Late in the afternoon, Spinner's wife, Gertrude, stopped in. She said she needed to shop for a dress and had come by to pick up some extra cash from the register in case she needed it. She was a couple of years older than Spinner, and generally pale, from a heart condition, I think Spinner had mentioned, although I wasn't entirely clear how a heart condition could make a person pale.

Gertrude gave me a hug and said, "Take care of yourself, Jonathan." Had she sensed that something was wrong? Did I suddenly look like a criminal? If I did, would I change back to myself in time?

But the day passed without a ripple. Customers came and went, and then, because it was a Sunday, at around three in the afternoon the usual group of old guys trickled down to the basement for their regular meeting. There were about eight total, though generally not all of them showed up each week— health-related difficulties, was my guess. I couldn't figure it out. They would arrive one by one—never together—wearing berets, string ties, desert boots, and baggy trousers, and they never spoke to anyone: not to each other, not even to Spinner. They certainly didn't buy any yogurt. A couple of weeks earlier I'd given Spinner a questioning look as I watched them leave. "Don't sweat it, Jonathan," Spinner had said. "I just rent the space to them for their meetings. They don't cause trouble, and it helps out." He turned away to polish a metal smoothie container. Clearly, the old guys were not a subject for discussion.

Quitting time came. I walked home, once again giving the animal shelter a wide berth. Would I have to do this for the rest of my life? It seemed like a good idea. That night was a repeat of the previous one, though with slightly less anxiety. I pulled the covers over my head and eventually slept, though not well.

Monday night passed, and Tuesday, and Wednesday. In the weeks that followed I learned from newspaper accounts that the dog at the shelter had not been Buck at all but a vicious brute named Megamon, responsible for the deaths of countless cats and dogs, and the serious mauling of a UPS driver. Megamon, the article said, had only been awaiting the results of a rabies test before he was to be put down, while the actual Buck had been lying on the couch in the office of the shelter's director all that morning, eating liver snaps and playing video games. The Scout, sad to say, was never found, but the dog was killed a few days later (again, according to the papers) as he stalked a class of preschoolers who were walking on a field trip to a local nature refuge. He had, the article explained, developed a taste for human flesh. The only good result of all this was that the actual Buck, whatever degree of surliness he may have projected, seemed positively benign in the wake of Megamon, and so had been spared. Also, according to the article, the other good news was that the man I had struck had not died, but fortunately for both of us, his injuries were limited to complete memory loss.

Regarding the dog's playing chess, I must have been mistaken.

After what seemed to me forever, the attention of the media finally turned elsewhere. The calls for witnesses of the "massacre," as they had called it, diminished to a trickle and then ceased. My life, and my life at Mister Twisty's, slowly returned to not-quite-normal. I felt like one of those old dogs

I had seen on my day at the shelter—given a reprieve from the gas, but only a reprieve.

Three months passed. I began to relax, though I suppose I had never been what people call a "laid-back" individual. Was it something to do with my past? Possibly. My parents had been fond of traveling, and they often took me with them. As a result, something of their perpetual worry about train schedules and boats' sailing without them may have rubbed off. In the past, various women had told me I needed to "kick back" and unwind, but I was never sure exactly what they meant.

Spinner gave me a modest raise. I had a birthday, for which Gertrude bought me a pair of socks. I avoided the shelter, but the extra walking had an upside; I started to work off some of that complimentary yogurt. Still, something wasn't right. Was my more or less constant fear of being arrested starting to take its toll? Or had it somehow made me sensitive to invisible forces I had been unable to detect in the past? Certainly one of those forces, though not all that invisible, might have been the giant, prone to wobbling in high winds, Mister Twisty statue itself, perched atop the roof, depicted as if skiing down an imaginary slope, a pointy-nosed, lump-jawed, half-shaven thug with a swollen head and spindly arms and legs, his only relation to frozen yogurt that I could see being a hat that resembled an inverted yogurt cone. In even moderate winds he emitted an eerie groan, as if in pain.

On the other hand, if it wasn't the statue, my discomfort might have originated from the constant slight tremor of the tiled floor, presumably caused by the pumps and refrigeration equipment that labored steadily beneath us. I should have been used to both the statue and the trembling by then, but still they made me nervous. Or maybe after all, my uneasiness came from nothing more complicated than the perpetual chill of the place, natural enough for an establishment that sold frozen goods. Sure, that was it, I thought.

In the meantime the old guys collected and dispersed on successive Sundays as usual, each of them unlocking the door to the basement and then locking it behind himself. I began to think about the fact that while Spinner had never given me even a single key to Mister Twisty's, any one of these aging males could enter and leave as he pleased. There was certainly nothing mysterious about their old-guy attire of headgear and comfortable shoes, but their comings and goings still seemed odd. I kept meaning to bring up the subject again with Spinner, but the time was somehow never right.

In the absence of any additional information—and Spinner was not forthcoming in this regard—I speculated vaguely about drug deals; but the men who went down to the basement looked nothing like South Americans, or salt-encrusted speedboat captains from the Gulf of Mexico, or even strung-out jazz musicians. While not exactly unfriendly, these elderly visitors to Mister Twisty's seemed introspective, and indeed completely preoccupied with some matter, the nature of which I could not guess. Surely, I told myself, a man with a wife like Gertrude, a wife with health problems, would not endanger her well-being by becoming involved in something shady.

Would he?

Then late one summer Sunday night something happened. It had been an especially hot day, so the evening was warm as well, a condition that was very good for the frozen yogurt business. As you might guess, thanks to a prolonged flurry of cones, bowls, bars, and family packs, by closing time the store had made a healthy profit. Spinner, who was with me as usual, looked happy about all the money he pulled from the register, but he also seemed especially tired. It was late, so late that the lights in the other shops in the mall had long been turned off. Spinner put the bills into stacks, counted them, and wrote the totals on a pad. He then took all of the stacks, plus a lot of change, and stuffed everything into a canvas bag to take home with him. It was only after he had finished that he paused.

"You know, Jonathan," he said, coughing, and then, in a completely uncharacteristic gesture, he spit into an empty yogurt cup. "I think I'm coming down with one of those darned summer colds. Would you mind wiping down the counters and polishing the machines by yourself? Then you can lock up the place. If you'd like, you can come in an hour later tomorrow to make up for it. I'll call you in the morning and we can work things out."

Spinner wiped his nose, handed me his key ring, and left. "Sleep well," I yelled after him. "Give my best to Gertrude."

He waved back, possibly wobbling just a bit, and then I was alone. I looked out the dark window at the empty parking spaces in front of the pizza shop, the nail salon, Pets Incorporated, McReedy's Hardware, the thrift store, The Treasure Chest, and all the other stores. The diagonals that separated the places for cars looked like nothing so much as children, possibly Cub Scouts lying down with their arms at their sides as part of some emergency-preparedness exercise, waiting patiently for the doctors and nurses to finish up so they could go home and continue to be good citizens.

This was the first time ever that Spinner had trusted me with the keys to Mister Twisty's. I was feeling very tired myself and, for some reason, sad. From the basement I could hear the hum of the giant cooling machines as I sprayed Windex on the counters to wipe away the stickiness and rubbed down the swirl machines with chrome cleaner. I was just about to go home when I heard, or thought I heard, a difference in the intensity of the sound below me. For a moment it occurred to me that I might be coming down with a cold myself, or maybe the flu; but when I shook my head and pressed my sinuses everything seemed fine. It was probably nothing, I thought, but what if there had been some kind of malfunction in the equipment downstairs . . . a fire . . . or what if one of the old guys had had a heart attack and fallen into the machinery? We never really kept track of who went down and who came back up. For all I knew there might have been an old man, someone's grandpa, down there at that very moment, dying. A few weeks earlier Spinner had said he'd been working on the equipment and it might still be not exactly right, but when he hired me he had told me never to go down to the basement for any reason.

On the other hand, if there wasn't an old guy dying down there, what *would* there be? Did these old men, as do so many of their kind, play chess? Would there be a chessboard, a timer, and a bathroom for tricky prostates? Would there be drugs and, if so, what sort would appeal to men so old they sometimes seemed barely able to push open the heavy glass front door of Mister Twisty's? I imagined an ordinary kitchen table, lit by a single bulb. Across the table's surface would be piles of laxatives and virility enhancers, with maybe a scale for weighing out their doses. I had no great objection to drugs—after all, yogurt was *a sort* of drug—but I had to be careful. If what was down there was against the law, it would mean that I'd have to decide whether to turn Spinner in or not. Ethical questions aside, it seemed like a good idea to avoid contact with the law for as long as I could. But if there *weren't* drugs, then what *were* those old guys doing down there in their clubhouse amid the compressors and freezers, cartons of cones, and boxes of gummy worms and sugar sprinkles?

I decided that I should check it out. If everything was fine, I wouldn't even have to mention it.

I searched Spinner's ring of keys until I found one that seemed to match the lock. It was small and silver, with a surprisingly pleasant, roundish head. I walked over to the door, aimed it at the lock—and *whoosh*, the key entered as if sucked in by a vacuum. I turned it and drew the door toward me. The noise of the machinery hit my ears; the door was a lot thicker than I would have guessed, and the machinery sounded powerful enough to explain, to some degree, the vibrations in the floor.

I assumed that there was a light switch at the top of the stairs, but I didn't need it. There was a faint glow coming from the bottom, so, with one hand touching the smooth plaster wall to my right, I walked carefully down the creaking wooden steps.

At the foot of the stairs I was surprised to find that the dull yellow glow came not, as I'd imagined, from a bare bulb suspended from the ceiling, but rather from the walls and corners, from what looked like giant, softly glowing Popsicles. To my surprise, the basement itself was far larger than the entire yogurt parlor above, and must have stretched at least to McReedy's Hardware, possibly even beneath Pets Incorporated, at the far corner of the mall. The stairs from Mister Twisty's appeared to be the only entrance or exit to the place, and as my eyes slowly grew accustomed to the light, I could see a cooling machine more grand than any I'd imagined—four or five times bigger than any refrigeration apparatus I'd ever seen in yogurt trade magazines, possibly ten times more powerful than would be necessary to supply a modest frozen-yogurt outlet such as Mister Twisty's.

Beneath and around the shadowy shape of the immense machine, I could just barely make out a mess of pipes and wires running along the floor, like the radii of a spider's web, connecting it to the tubes of glowing light. The whole effect was like sitting in the center of dark, medieval chapel, watching the sunset as it lit up a circle of dim and narrow stained-glass windows. It was beautiful and mysterious.

"Hello," I called out.

No one answered.

And I was just about to turn back and go upstairs when it occurred to me that I'd probably never again have the chance to take a really good look at all the stuff down there. The next morning, either cured of his sniffles or crammed full of over-the-counter cold medications, Spinner would reclaim his keys, and in the future he would lock up Mister Twisty's just as he had every night for the whole time I'd worked there, as I stood beside him watching, and the old guys would still come and go as they pleased.

This was the time, I decided, to take a better look at the glowing objects placed around the walls. I chose one set of pipes running out from the central compressor and followed it to a tall cylinder with a sort of burnished metal cap and a shiny metal base, out of which stuck four silver fins, strangely like those of the V-2 rockets that fell on London in newsreels from the Second World War. Or, to use a more modern analogy, it resembled a seven-foot-tall version of one of those fancy Italian espresso boilers you sometimes see in trendy coffee bars, hissing and wheezing out phlegmy portions of java. Between the base and the cap were about six feet of cloudy glass, or possibly Plexiglas.

I placed my hand against it and felt a slight hum, almost a pulse. As I moved my hand to the bottom of the cylinder, down between the fins, my fingertips inadvertently brushed against what felt like a toggle switch. I hesitated, wondering whether it might be connected to an alarm, but then I reasoned that you don't go around installing alarm switches in the hope that a burglar will deliberately set one off. My forefinger slipped under the smooth metal ball at its tip and flipped it upward. At first nothing happened. Then there was a flicker behind the glass, and slowly the faint glow brightened to reveal the form of a young and actual and completely naked woman.

The woman was blonde and somewhere in her twenties, I guessed, her pale hair floating like strands of egg white in the mysterious liquid that surrounded her, her blue eyes open wide and slightly crossed, her nose straight and thin, her breasts white and symmetrical, her knees knocked, her feet slender, with bluish veins running along their tops down to her toes like mountain streams pouring out of a glacier. The luminous fluid that enveloped her gave the hair follicles on her arms, lifted away from her skin, a special sheen, making it seem that she was lit from within as well as by the light. She had just the slightest overbite, and her nails were ragged; she must have chewed them in the past when she was nervous. I walked around the cylinder. There were no visible signs of violence to her body—no gunshot or stab wounds, and no discoloration around her neck that might have indicated strangulation. In fact, except that she couldn't possibly still be alive in that vat of who-knew-what, she didn't seem to be dead at all.

I looked around, feeling nervous. All at once I was aware that each one of the dimly glowing rocket/coffeemaker-type appliances that lined the walls might have a similar form waiting for me. A chill went down my back. I walked over to the next glowing tube, maybe three yards away, and found and flipped the toggle switch. Once again the light flickered and the glass slowly grew brighter to reveal another naked woman, a beautiful black-haired young lady with thin wrists and ankles, skin the color of toast when the toaster is set on THREE, and long, slender toes and fingers. I imagined her to be a Latina, though of course I had no way of knowing for certain. Then, as if I were in the middle of a complicated dream, I walked from cylinder to cylinder, turning on the light of each to reveal its contents. My fears proved only too well founded. Each cylinder contained a woman: the blonde, the Latina, an Asian, a dark-skinned woman, and, set slightly apart from the rest, one who looked like an Eskimo (Inuit, I think, is the correct term), all young and all waiting for something.

But what?

Without knowing when exactly I had begun, I found myself pacing like an animal caught in a cage, in tighter and tighter circles, until I began to get dizzy and realized that all my walking was stirring up a fair amount of dust. *Stop*, I told myself. Slow down. You don't want to start coughing; it might attract someone (though I couldn't imagine who would hear me). Then I spotted one last (at least I hoped it was the last) cylinder partly hidden behind the stairwell, next to a pile of cardboard file boxes. I walked over and flipped on its light.

I took a breath.

And another.

My God, I thought . . .

But how could *that* be?

Because although it was true that the woman behind the glass looked exactly like my very first girlfriend, Mary Katherine—had the same auburn hair with a neat widow's peak; the same tiny ears (I squinted to see whether this woman's ears were pierced, as Mary Katherine's had been, but couldn't be sure); Mary Katherine's delicate mouth and Mary Katherine's crimson lips, now forever moistened by that mysterious fluid surrounding her; Mary Katherine's feathery eyebrows, which nearly touched; Mary Katherine's kneecaps, as sweet as two porcelain teacups; and Mary Katherine's breasts, still fresh, still plump and desirable—this particular woman could not possibly be the same Mary Katherine that I'd known a dozen years ago, precisely because this woman looked so very much like the frozen picture in my memory. My mind spun like a racing car out of control and then, coming into the straightaway out of the far turn, flipped over once, twice, hit the wall, burst into acrid flames right in front of the grandstand, taking out three rows of the high-priced seats along with it.

It was by the light of those flames that I examined the woman once again. It seemed obvious: if she *were* Mary Katherine, and not just some fantasy, surely she would *have* to have aged, just as I had over the years. I'd lost muscle tone, a little hair, and even some flexibility in my joints, which had caused me some disappointment a few weeks earlier when I failed to qualify for the Mall Employees' Bowling Team. And I was still in my thirties. I hated to think what was still to come. I had also accumulated wrinkles, occasional indigestion, and a tic in my left eye when I was nervous, one I could feel coming on at that very moment. But this version of Mary Katherine floating before me now was *exactly the same*, given, of course, that nobody's memory is all that good over time. For example, there was a small mole over this woman's right hip bone, and I couldn't be positive if Mary Katherine's mole had been on the right or the left side, or even, to tell the truth, that Mary Katherine had actually *had* a mole. For that matter, I suppose it was possible that the mole had in reality belonged to some-one else I'd known, and in some slip of that old paste brush I had glued it onto Mary Katherine in the messy scrapbook of my memory. If only I had had a photo I might have been able to check, but because I had believed our love together would last a lifetime, I had disdained such crude mementos.

But without a photo, how could I be sure? If Mary Katherine could have spoken at that moment— "How are you, Jonathan? I'd hoped I'd never see you again as long as I lived"—the answer would have been simple, but without even a gesture there was no way to tell who this woman was.

So I just stood there like some kind of boob in front of what they used to call the boob tube and stared at my own reflection, darkened and smeared by the curving glass as it stretched around this woman's all-too-familiar form, and I listened to the sound of the compressors as they compressed not just the gas that cooled the cylinders, but time itself. Then from behind me I heard a cough, and for a moment I had the wild thought that one of the women had suddenly come to life and in a minute would be asking for my help.

"Surely," the voice behind me said, "you didn't think I would forget to install a silent alarm system, did you?"

3

I turned to see a man about my own height and weight and about twenty years older than me, wearing a beige trench coat covered with what looked to be yogurt stains. Beneath the coat poked out two striped pajama-bottom legs and two fuzzy blue slippers, and out of one sleeve protruded a largish revolver that was trained on me. He looked tired, with his hair puffed out on one side, as if he'd been sleeping on the other half, but he also looked excited, cranky, and he was Spinner. I stared at the fat tips of the shining bullets nestled in their chambers, tiny sisters of those grown-up cylinders around me, aimed exactly at my heart.

"Spinner," I said, "I hope you can believe that my being here is entirely out of concern for your interests. I thought . . ."

"I thought I told you," he said, "never to come down here, and now you're here. This means I shall have to kill you, which to be honest I don't want to do, at least not yet." He took a red handkerchief from the left pocket of his trench coat and blew his nose.

I was about to tell him that I was in complete agreement with his nonviolent principles and therefore, if it was all the same to him, we could just pretend it never happened; but before I had the chance, he gestured with his gun toward a stack of folding chairs I had failed to notice leaning against a wall. "Why don't you set up a couple of those, Jonathan, so you and I can have a talk." He pointed toward a wooden table, much like the one I'd imagined the old guys hunkering around, that I also hadn't noticed.

As I worked to get the chairs open—they were complicated in some way I was having trouble understanding—I studied the features of the man who had recently trusted me with the keys to Mister Twisty's. They had not changed from less than an hour earlier—the runny nose, the close-set eyes, the heavy jaw beneath a skull that narrowed like a mountain to an almost majestic peak, very like the shape of my own head, in fact—but on his face was an expression I had never seen before, a combination of paranoia, power, and resentment of having to get out of bed to return to the store when he wasn't feeling his best.

Spinner sat down and, to his credit, seemed to search for a place to begin. "I've never been in a situation quite like this, Jonathan, though I've certainly considered it a possibility for some time now," he said. "Therefore, while I'm trying to decide how to dispose of the matter of your being down here, let me tell you a little story that you may find of interest. It may help me make up my mind." He sat for a minute, his pistol still trained at my center, collecting his facts. "I don't know whether you've ever had a cat, but I once did, and I loved that cat more than you could ever know."

"That's really great," I said. "People who like animals are the best kind of people around."

Spinner gave me a look. "Shut up," he continued. "Maybe I loved her too much, because I used to take her everywhere with me—this was before I met Gertrude, so there was no one to leave her with. The fact is that I even brought her here, to Mister Twisty's, where, because of health regulations, I'd keep her in the basement while I worked upstairs; but every hour or two I'd pop down and rub her back or scratch her belly, which she really liked."

"That was nice of you." I wondered if his finding me in the basement had possibly unhinged him.

Spinner's features darkened. "Listen, Jonathan," he said, "I'm trying to explain what it is you're seeing around you, so pay attention. One afternoon we got very busy; it was a scorcher, like today, and it seemed as if I'd done nothing but serve yogurt for five hours straight, clear into dinnertime, when I remembered I'd left Sparkles down here, all alone."

"Sparkles," I said. "What kind of name is that for a cat?"

Spinner laid the gun on the table, but kept three fingers resting just between the cylinder and the handle, as if he were taking my measure.

"It was a very good name," he said, "because when she was in the sun her fur, which was white, got kind of sparkly. So I came down here and called and called, but there was no answer. I poked around and found nothing. Because she was a white cat, she should have been easy to spot, but try as I might I couldn't find a single trace of her anywhere." He paused. "I could only assume that Sparkles had somehow found a way out on her own."

I nodded at Spinner. "I'm kind of a dog person myself," I said, "but I can certainly see how upsetting a thing like that would be."

Spinner wiped his nose, which was starting to drip. "I never got over it," he said. "And though people told me I should go to the animal shelter and pick out a new one, I just couldn't think about any other cat but Sparkles."

At the mention of the shelter I could feel my eye twitch, but Spinner seemed not to notice.

"Then one day, a couple of weeks after Sparkles disappeared, I was down here by the sink"—Spinner pointed to a sink I hadn't noticed—"pouring some left-over yogurt into a barrel I kept around for that purpose—every couple of months a farmer would pick it up to feed to his pigs—when I saw at the bottom what looked like a huge lump of fudge. But I couldn't remember putting any fudge in there, and its shape kind of reminded me of something else, something I had pushed all the way to the back of my mind. I reached in the barrel and lifted it out, then laid it in the sink, where I began to hose it off, and you know what I found? It was Sparkles—dead, of course—but here's the thing: she was perfectly preserved, without a sign of mold or decay or rot. Except for the fact she wasn't moving, she looked almost like a kitten again. Anyway, I wrapped her in some paper towels and took her out back and left her in the Dumpster. I have to admit at that precise moment I was much too upset over her death to deal with the implications of what had happened; but then the next day I got to thinking. What was in this yogurt stuff, I asked myself, that could act as such a great preservative?"

"Yes," I said, "it's so often true, isn't it, that for all the controlled scientific experimentation that goes on in this world, the most important discoveries often come about completely by accident, and it's equally true that in many of those cases our animal friends play a major role."

"Shut up," Spinner repeated. "So anyway, for a long time I thought about what might have gone on with Sparkles. I'd read, as I'm sure you have, all those news reports about Bulgarians living to a hundred and seventy or a hundred and eighty years old as a result of the yogurt in their diet, and so I began to put two and two together. Suppose, I thought, that in addition to digesting food, the special bacteria in yogurt might actually digest those poisons in our bodies that cause aging and decay. And then I thought a little more: suppose that after removing the milk solids, an intelligent person could make a solution of those enzyme-producing bacteria that would be so powerful that as long as a body was submerged in them it would never die, but sleep, waiting only for someone with the proper skill and knowledge to wake it."

"And?"

"And, Jonathan, one thing led to another. I tried this and that on various forms of life, with mixed results—I won't bore you with the details, although I have to say I could definitely see some progress. My first attempt on an actual person, however, was a sort of humanitarian gesture. It so happened that I had a colleague in the yogurt business who was getting on in years, and his wife was, too. One day he told me that she had been diagnosed with a terminal disease and had only weeks to live. He was pretty broken up of course, so I told him about Sparkles and my experiments. I explained to him that I hadn't exactly brought anyone back from the treatment, but he said that didn't matter so much to him. He said he loved her so much that he'd like to try to keep her alive until a cure was found. But then, unfortunately, just at the time a cure *was* found, he died, and when I tried to revive his wife so that she could attend his memorial service it didn't work. I don't know why—maybe because she wasn't healthy in the first place. But here's the thing: before her husband died he must have talked to somebody, because more or less out of the blue fathers started bringing in their daughters, and uncles their nieces, who, they said, just needed to buy a little time until a cure for whatever terminal diseases they had could be found. Naturally I told them I couldn't absolutely promise I'd be able to revive them when the right moment came, and that setting up these cylinders and so on wasn't cheap, but I guess when people are desperate they'll try anything, and so I kept getting new customers. The thing is, though, that with every new person, with each failure—and there were quite a few, a lot of them actually—I kept increasing the base of my knowledge."

"And the old guys?" I asked. "How did they get into the act?"

"The old guys just sort of evolved. I don't know how," Spinner said. "At first it was just one of the uncles who brought along a friend to keep him company, then others followed. At first they were a comfort to family members who came to visit their loved ones while they waited for a cure, and then they took on kind of a life of their own, so that even when the family members lost interest, which was more often than you'd think, the old guys would still show up Sundays right on schedule. I said it was a kind of a club, didn't I?"

Spinner reached in his coat for his handkerchief and gave his nose a good hard blow. He should be getting some rest, I thought. "You know," he continued, "about those places that cut off your head and then keep it frozen for you on the chance that one day somebody will figure out how to stick it on again. Which would you prefer, Jonathan, that, or letting your head stay right where it is, surrounded by yogurt?"

"But these women?" I gestured around me. "Surely *they* aren't suffering from any kind of disease or anything," I said. "They look extremely healthy."

"That's more complicated," Spinner said. He paused, as if he were thinking. "You're correct, however; they're not the same as the sickly ones I started with."

The tension, or something in the basement air, caused me to let out an involuntary yawn.

"By the way, I'm not boring you, am I?" Spinner asked, picking up the revolver again. "Because if I am, I can certainly finish this off quickly."

"On the contrary," I told him, and added that if I appeared weary it was only because I had stayed up most of the previous night thinking about ways to make Mister Twisty's more profitable. "I have several very good ideas," I said, "that I'll be happy to share with you at another time. But you were going to tell me about these women who are here now. How did they get here if they weren't brought in by their dads and uncles and such?"

Spinner thought some more. "Listen, Jonathan," he said, "it's true that's how it all started. But lately other people have gotten involved with this. Important people I can't talk about right now. Something as big as this could be—it's hard to keep it completely quiet. Maybe later, if things work out, I'll fill you in."

I allowed myself to feel the cool breeze of hope as it brushed across my forehead. For the first time I allowed myself to believe I might survive this night. But even if I didn't, I still had to know: "And these women around us, are they or aren't they dying?"

He relaxed a notch. "Well, no. The thing is that the main problem with the first women was that they weren't very healthy to begin with, and the yogurt, instead of arresting the disease, for some reason or another seems to preserve the body while allowing the disease to keep on going. So saving people with a terminal disease was only phase one, if you can follow me, because it didn't work very well at all. These women are more like phase two, a whole new story, and believe me, when we switched from sick people to healthy ones, it made all the difference."

"*We?*"

"Yes, we," Spinner answered. "As I told you, this current project has far-reaching implications, and there are only a couple of relatively minor bugs that remain to be worked out. My principals are waiting for me to let them know when it's time to move to phase three, which will be the really big phase. Actually they're getting a little anxious. But all you need to know is that these women here are basically what you might call volunteers . . . entrepreneurs . . . pioneers . . . like those people who are first in line to test some new cancer drug or antibiotic." Spinner was waving his arms at this point, and the gun was still in one of them.

"But with drugs don't you just take a pill? Isn't this entirely different?"

"In a way, yes, but you don't think that taking penicillin—which, in its own fashion, is as natural as acidophilus, by the way—was always as simple as taking a pill, do you? Listen Jonathan, you don't have to worry about these women. Some of them, I was told, come from poor families and are simply trying to make the best of a bad situation. These women know that they're making an investment in their future, because when they eventually come back to life, they'll be rich. It's some kind of stock-option or retirement thing. It's like taking a really long ocean cruise, and by the time they get back from it they'll find that their investment portfolios have gone through the roof."

"And what about the ones before these women? Have you ever actually revived anyone? Has anyone ever come back out of this . . . state, I guess you'd call it?"

"Not exactly," Spinner said. "But that's ancient history, as they say. For the women around us, you have to realize this is money in the bank; the longer they wait, the more they'll have. If something is working don't fix it, is my motto."

Spinner's eyes were starting to water pretty badly, and for a second it occurred to me that he might shoot me then and there just so he could get back into bed. I pushed the thought away and, thankfully, he continued. "I didn't mention it, but these women down here have contracts. I haven't actually read them, but I'm told they're very generous."

Did I believe Spinner was telling the truth? Honestly, it was hard to know what to think. Some of it made sense and some none at all, but I had always read that in any hostage situation, the important thing was to keep the captor talking. Here was a situation, that was for certain, and if I wasn't a hostage, then what was I?

"That all sounds really reasonable," I told him, "but just for the sake of argument, couldn't a person say those old guys are kind of taking advantage of them in the meantime? And what is with this one-of-every-kind business? Is this supposed to be like an exhibit at the Museum of Natural History? I'll grant you that these women knew what they were signing on for, but don't you suppose that, if we could ask them now what their choice would be, at least one of them might change her mind? Don't you think an unbiased observer might say they deserve the chance?"

"Listen, Jonathan," Spinner crossed his legs. "I can't give you many details about these women, but if it's their lack of clothing that's bothering you, I can tell you that acidophilus, no matter how good it may be for flesh, is really hard on fabric." He took out the red handkerchief and blew his nose again.

Something had shifted in the balance of power. An invisible ball bearing had rolled across the table toward me. Whether in time it would reverse its course and roll back toward Spinner, I couldn't guess.

"Now don't get all self-righteous on me, Jonathan," Spinner said. "Are you telling me that you've never checked out one of those so-called girlie magazines? Or if not, haven't you ever been at the barber's and leafed through a respectable athletic journal that just happened to have an issue devoted to women in swimsuits? You don't really believe those pictures are about swimming, do you? You do get your hair cut, no? Or maybe you've flipped through the daily newspaper on your way to an article about a plane crash but paused for a moment at an advertisement showing a woman standing around in her underwear? What do you think that's all about? The underwear? And out of all the women in those advertisements, wouldn't you guess that a couple of years after her picture was taken at least one of them might have changed *her* mind? But it's too late, isn't it? The ads are out there. The promotion has already taken place and all that underwear has either been sold or not. That's history, too. And speaking of history, do you ever replay in your memory scenes with women you yourself once knew? You're not going to tell me you never dated a woman, are you, Jonathan? Some woman whom maybe you haven't thought about for years, and then suddenly something reminds you of her . . ."

I fought not to look at the one I called Mary Katherine slowly bobbing behind him and stared instead at the Asian woman with her finely sculpted features, her taut body, her close-cropped black hair, and her blank and inward gaze. It suddenly occurred to me that *she* reminded me of a girl I knew in grammar school, whose name I had long forgotten, but who had been kind to me once in the cafeteria as other students pelted me with the remains of their lunches. "Pay them no mind, Jonathan," she had said to me with the wisdom of a culture that reached far beyond the petty revenge-oriented strategies of the Occident. "Beneath the great eye of heaven all things pale to insignificance."

But Spinner seemed to be on a roll. "And of course those ex-girlfriends of yours may well despise you now—women always have their reasons, don't they, Jonathan? But does that give them some kind of automatic copyright on themselves? Who among us has the right to issue a cease-and-desist order anytime we want just to prevent someone else from thinking about us? You? Me? The Supreme Court? I don't think so."

I had to admit I hadn't really given this matter much thought, and what's more, it also seemed that Spinner was beginning to enjoy himself, which was kind of a relief.

"So what's the difference," he continued, "between these women around us now, and a snapshot, say, taken by a casual photographer of any woman at all on a street? The woman on the street doesn't know her picture has been taken. These women you're looking at can't see us sitting here looking at them and talking about them because at this moment, Jonathan, they're nowhere; they're in dreamland. When they do come back to life, they'll be richer than you or I will ever be, and maybe even grateful. What about all those women who marry old millionaires and actually have to spend time with them while they're waiting for them to kick off? They have to listen to the old guy wheeze getting into bed every night and wake up smelling his farts. Which would you pick? I'm sure even you have to admit that this is a big step up for women's rights, opportunistically speaking."

"But wait a minute," I said. "How can you be so sure they truly wanted to come down here? How about that one"—I pointed to Mary Katherine—"for example?"

"Honestly," Spinner said, "I can't give you a guarantee. But just you think about it: for these women, not a moment has passed since they stepped off the conveyer belt of time. They'll stay young while everyone around them, you and me included, will just get older. How many people would die for that to happen, not even including that package of stock options I mentioned earlier?"

Spinner lifted the revolver and waved it around. "So it seems that you're fond of women, are you?"

Was he going to shoot me? My stomach made a hideous sound all on its own.

"If you kill me down here, there'll be a mess," I said. "And don't forget that the police, or someone, will come looking for me. I'm not like these poor girls. I've got friends." Technically speaking, this last part wasn't true, but it seemed no time to split hairs; besides, the first part, about the police, more than made up for it.

Spinner looked at me. A surprisingly warm, even slightly humorous smile began to find its way onto his face. "Sure you do, Jonathan, sure you do. It may interest you to know that the only real friend you have is me. And it's not just that you remind me of myself in so many ways—the real reason I've decided to let you live is because of something else entirely."

I suppose I must have looked confused, or it may have been in reaction to my nervousness over the situation, but Spinner laughed. "Jonathan," he said, "you don't think I would keep any employee above such a delicate environment as the basement of Mister Twisty's without checking his background first?"

No, I told myself. *It can't be.*

"Now think a little more," Spinner said. "Even if you went to the police and reported what you see all around you, as I told you, these women signed contracts, and the case would be tied up in the courts for years. In fact, once the news of my acidophilus breakthrough is made public, I might even be in line for a grant from the National Institutes of Health. But you, Jonathan . . . let me mention just one name in the hope that it may get your attention. Are you ready?"

I nodded.

"Elberta," he said, and I thought I could feel my heart stop in my chest.

"But how . . . ?"

"Never mind," Spinner said. "You get my point."

I did. Elberta was the woman I had met after I had lost Mary Katherine, and to say that things had not turned out well would be a considerable understatement.

The handkerchief came out and Spinner blew his nose hard. He looked as if he really, really could use a rest. "Listen," he said. "It's been a long evening, and right now we've both been through a lot. What do you say we call it a night? Trudy would be sad if you disappeared, and, frankly, I'd miss you too. I've come to enjoy your company more than I thought I would when you first came to work. Besides, I may have plans for you in the future. Suppose you keep quiet about what you know, and I will too. I'll tell Trudy this was just a false alarm. You won't speak of the girls again unless I bring it up. Agreed?"

"I agree," I answered. "I certainly will not."

"I'll see you tomorrow," Spinner said, and added, "but you should know that if you ever change your mind, I've left envelopes with details of the Elberta episode in certain places. If anything happens to me, you may well find yourself in considerable embarrassment, if you get my drift. Nor will you enter this basement unless I ask you to. Is that understood?"

What choice did I have? And after all, those girls weren't my responsibility, were they? I mean, I wasn't the one who put them there. By going down to the basement in the first place I was only trying to be helpful.

We shook hands on it.

4

That night, after Spinner and I parted and I finally went to bed, I dreamed of Mary Katherine for the first time in years. She was wearing nothing but a cigar wrapper, and although she was trying to speak, no words came out of her deliciously sensuous mouth.

I'd met Mary Katherine back when I was still at State College, back when I was full of hope, when I was still young. She was my first real love, the first girl I ever really dated before I met Elberta. During those years I had no idea what I wanted to do with my life; I only knew that in some small way I wanted to help all of mankind, maybe animals, too, and be remembered. How I got from college to the yogurt parlor in St. Nils is a long story, one that spirals mostly downhill following Elberta. But back then at State College I asked myself, as so many others had before me, what I could do that would really make a difference. And maybe it was to answer this question that I had gotten into the habit of attending a weekly series of memorials for extinct animals sponsored by the Extinction Club. The purpose of these gatherings was to make people more conscious of the fragile condition of the environment and the general precariousness of all the species that share this planet with us.

We would meet at night, each of us holding a candle in a darkened room of the business building, and sit in front of a picture of whatever extinct animal we chose to celebrate that week. As we gazed at its likeness, pinned to a bulletin board, various people contributed what bits of information they had researched about the animal's size and habitat, its preferences and enemies, in short, what used to constitute a typical day in its life, in much the same way one remembers an old friend at a wake. "He used to love sucking the heads off baby birds," one might say; or "He'd walk for hours each night from tree to tree, making his mark along the base of every one."

Following this mournful recollection of a life-form we would never have the chance to meet, a club member would be chosen to take on the role of the Last Animal of Its Kind. One by one we would exit the room, until only the animal's representative was left. At that point, whoever the spokesperson was would deliver his or her farewell address: the final message that the last member of its species would have spoken to our species, if it could have. We listened through the open doorway, standing silently in the hall. Interestingly, these monologues were mostly not so much full of recrimination and anger, although the animals in question, we pretty much agreed, were certainly entitled to that, but instead tended toward sad warnings to our own species to avoid their fate. And more often than not, the person chosen to deliver such a speech was Mary Katherine.

How could I not fall in love?

To make a long story short, when a meeting of the Extinction Club was halted halfway through because of a bomb threat later found to have been phoned in by a member of the Entrepreneurs Club who resented our using business department facilities, I took Mary Katherine out for coffee. From the coffeehouse, still under the spell of bongo drums and a lone guitar, we retired to her apartment, where we made love, and for weeks afterward we laughed together, felt sad together, mourned extinct species together. We went on long trips to the zoo. We drove to the donut shop and back. We created pet names. Mine was Honey Balloon and hers was Rub-a-Dub. Don't ask why. I swore to protect her always, and she vowed to support me just as soon as I decided on a direction for my career. Then one day a handsome Frenchman appeared as a special guest to deliver the final speech of the dodo, which had perished on his country's soil, so to speak, in Mauritius.

"Allo, allo," he said, speaking through a paper tube that was supposed to imitate a dodo's bill. "I have no more friends to rub against. I am lone-ly. I call my call: allo, allo, but no-body answer."

Standing in the hall next to Mary Katherine, I saw her lips form a silent "Allo" back.

Following that night's meeting, Mary Katherine said she wanted to walk home alone because she had a headache, and the day after that I got a message on my answering machine. "I won't be seeing you again," Mary Katherine said. "I've decided to complete my studies at the Sorbonne."

By the time I returned her call, her number was already out of service.

Sometimes, when I went to the zoo, I would look around at the crowd surrounding an exhibit or a popcorn stand to see if she'd returned, with or without the Frenchman, but I never found a trace of her. Now I was faced with her double.

Needless to say, there was no sleeping in the next day, and after I arrived at Mister Twisty's, when I wasn't waiting on customers, I spent most of the time watching Spinner. His cold was a lot worse, so much so that at least three customers, after he had given them their orders, took one look at him, then at their cones, and deposited them untouched in the trash can outside. All that day I thought more about Mary Katherine. I had moved several times since my college days. Suppose she had been trying to contact me?

The following morning I was woken by the ringing of my phone. It was Gertrude. "Good morning," she said. "I'm sorry to get you up like this, Jonathan, but Spinner is really sick today. Do you suppose that as a personal favor to me you could go into Mister Twisty's, open up, and stay at least until he can arrive there himself? He told me to wake him, but a couple of extra hours of sleep would do him a world of good, and I'm sure he'll make it up to you. I have to go out for a while, but if you can stop by right away, I'll give you the keys."

Was this a test of some sort? Ordinarily Spinner made it a point to arrive at least an hour before the place opened, and had me come in even after that. Now I knew why he had wanted that time, of course—to check on the women. "OK," I said, "I'll be happy to swing by on the way to work."

When I arrived at Mister Twisty's, I let myself in with

the keys that Gertrude gave me, the same set Spinner had entrusted to me so recently. The first thing I noticed, to my surprise, was that the key to the basement had not been removed. Did this mean that Spinner was really, seriously, sick, too sick even to take the most simple precaution against my returning there, or was it a trap? Had he reset the alarm, and was he sitting at home right now, waiting for me to go downstairs again, at which time he would pick up the phone to call the unnamed powers he had spoken about, the sponsors of the women in the basement? I didn't begrudge Spinner his rest. He *had* looked terrible the previous day, and I was still in the mode of being grateful to be alive. I took care of the lunch crowd by myself, but you could hardly call it a crowd. It was light because the day was chilly, and for once I was happy about the lack of business.

The hours passed, and at any minute I expected the front door of Mister Twisty's to open and Spinner to announce his arrival, but by two in the afternoon he still hadn't shown. He must be extremely sick, I thought, and I even felt a little guilty for getting him out of bed two nights ago. A well-dressed lady came in, bought a quart of Marshmallow Madness, and left. The sky grew dark, and the wrought-iron fixtures in the shop took on the clumsy and lethal look of instruments of torture. The shop stayed empty and outside it looked like rain. I pulled up a heavy black chair and sat near the front, staring out the window at the parking lot as cars came and left. McReedy's Hardware was having a sale on tarps, and it seemed to be a success. Still, it felt strange to be there at that moment, with it about to rain here in the real world, in the world of time, knowing that below me the same Mary Katherine (or was it?) I'd been dreaming of only hours ago was bobbing far, far beyond the reach of human clocks in her glass cylinder filled with a clear solution of acidophilus. Nothing in my life till then had ever prepared me for such a situation.

It was all I could do to keep from posting a back-in-fifteen-minutes sign in the front window and dashing downstairs to see whether the other night had been only a crazy dream, or rather a nightmare, but I resisted. Still, my mind seemed unable to leave alone the question of how, if it was Mary Katherine, she had gotten there. Had she acquired a drug habit, and was she waiting either until she had enough money to support it in comfort, or until society would come to its collective senses and realize that it was costing far more resources to enforce this unenforceable prohibition than it would be to simply make the drugs legal, and possibly even pay people to take them? Certainly, the civic cost alone, to say nothing of the potential goodwill of addicts lost through estrangement and alienation, which in turn prevented them from adding their voices to the cause of honest government, was staggering.

But if Mary Katherine had needed money, why hadn't she contacted me? Had she tried? Had she been ashamed of her addiction? Was she embarrassed to have left me for a Frenchman? Alternately, had a degree from the Sorbonne made her too proud to ask for help from a non-Francophone? I wasn't wealthy, but I would have come to her aid in a moment. Or once again, perhaps Spinner was lying, and the women, Mary Katherine included, were not volunteers at all but victims, picked off by the unscrupulous syndicate hinted at by Spinner, which, using a drug-laced cappuccino, had tossed them like sacks of coffee beans into the back of an unmarked van, and then prepared them in some ghastly way for the vat of acidophilus. Had Spinner been involved in that acquisition stage of the operation? He had been noticeably vague on those details.

But of course, I told myself, that woman wasn't really Mary Katherine. How could it be?

Two men in dark, well-tailored suits came into Mister Twisty's, and my heart sank. Had Spinner turned me in? Was he only pretending to be sick at home during my arrest? If he had, I couldn't blame him. Had I been set up by Gertrude while Spinner was in his bed recuperating? On second thought, from everything I could tell, Gertrude knew nothing about what was going on in the basement. Outside, it looked as if there was a chance that the rain might blow over and that St. Nils's famously changeable weather would score yet another upset. For a moment I considered feigning the need for something from the rear of the shop, and then fleeing out the back door, but I decided to stay, and to my relief each man ordered a Tropical Fruit Surprise double cone. "We need to talk to Spinner," the taller one said. "Is he here?"

"No," I told them, and in a burst of gratitude that I'd been spared twice in twenty-four hours, I added that Spinner was probably still sleeping in; he was under the weather, I said, but would probably be fine tomorrow. If it was really an emergency, they could try him where he lived. "Is he expecting you?" I asked.

"Yes," one said.

"No," the other said at the same time, but he added, "I mean, he's expecting us, and we thought we would find him here. We have some really, really good news, and Spinner will be angry if he hears we stopped by to see him and you didn't give us his address."

I wrote it down. "Keep ringing the bell," I said. "He could be hard to wake."

They looked at each other and then at me, nodded once, and left.

I briefly thought of calling Spinner to tell him that some guys who were looking for him had stopped by. "It was strange," I might have told him. "They both ordered Tropical Fruits on a cool day like this, when most people want chocolate. How often does that happen? You might want to keep an eye out to see whether they turn up." But then a salesman came by, wanting us to increase the size of our ad in the phone directory, and it took me a while to convince him that it wasn't my responsibility. When he settled for a free cone and left, I decided that Spinner had probably been expecting the men at Mister Twisty's and had just forgotten his appointment. If I called I'd only be tying up the phone for nothing. Spinner was probably sleeping off his cold, and every minute of rest counted. I didn't want to tip the scales of our new understanding at such an early stage; Spinner could be vindictive, I knew. I went back to leaning on the counter and staring out the window.

The shop remained empty. I wiped down all the counters and the chairs, and even cleaned the glass of the front door, which tended to smudge. Then I walked outside to spot any approaching customers. The sun had come out, but the whole mall was as deserted as Mister Twisty's. Apparently McReedy had sold his last tarp. It would be a good time, I told myself, to clean out the shelves beneath the counter where we kept the straws and napkins and yogurt cups. More than once during peak periods at Mister Twisty's I had found myself wasting valuable time stuffing boxes back where they had fallen from, or moving things around to reach some needed item while a customer was waiting. So I stooped behind the counter and began to work. Then, finding the position awkward, I sat on the floor until, exhausted by the drama of late, and without knowing exactly how it happened, I found myself lying down, and I fell asleep.

How long I slept I do not know, but I was awakened by the bang of the front door being opened rapidly and with too much force. I quickly stood, and there, staring at me across the familiar counter, was Spinner, who, I had to admit, looked pretty bad.

Worse than bad, in fact. In an instant it was clear that he had been horribly beaten: one arm stuck out at a disturbing angle, his clothing was shredded, his skin was raw and bleeding, several teeth were nowhere to be seen, and one eye was completely shut. How had he ever made it as far as Mister Twisty's?

"Spinner," I said, "what happened?"

"They found me," he managed to say before he died.

5

Much of what followed I suppose you will find familiar from watching cop shows on television: I immediately called Gertrude; the police came and sealed off Mister Twisty's with that same yellow tape I remembered so vividly from my morning at the animal shelter; the officers asked if I had seen any sinister-looking strangers hanging around; and when I described the two men who had come by earlier, they took fingerprints. Finding none but mine, because I had inadvertently wiped the place clean, they helped themselves to several cups of swirled yogurt. Finally they went back to the station, or somewhere else. They would get back to me, they said.

I didn't dare tell the police about the basement, for the obvious reason that they would assume I had something to do with the presence of those poor women. I washed the blood and fluids from the area by the front door, plus all that black fingerprint powder, which was really worse than anything, and finally went home to my apartment.

I was awakened shortly after midnight by Gertrude, who had taken a taxi and appeared to be slightly disoriented by the meds her doctor had prescribed following the news of

Spinner's death. She was paler than ever, her hair in curlers and her eyes red from weeping, but I was relieved to see that she had the look of a survivor. There was a spot of lotion on one of her temples, and she was holding out a plate of peanut butter cookies covered in plastic wrap. "I'm sorry. I couldn't sleep," she said. "So I found myself doing what I always do when I get anxious. I bake." She removed the wrap. "But then, when I looked for someone to give it to, Claude was gone, and the truth is I needed to talk. I'm sure Claude never discussed this—it wasn't his way—but he was very fond of you. So I had these cookies, and then I thought that Claude would want you to have them. They were his favorite, and he used to say, 'Gertrude, you bake the best peanut butter cookies in the world.' I hope you like peanut butter cookies. I know they aren't to everyone's taste."

"Gertrude," I told her, "thank you. That is so nice of you at a difficult time like this."

She looked at me and snuffled for a second. "Why don't you try one?"

I had a cookie, and then another. The fact was that peanut butter cookies were my least favorite cookies in the universe; you could even say I disliked them, but it seemed no time for candor. "These are great," I told her. "I can't believe that with all this pressure you could still . . ."

She interrupted. "It's so strange, Jonathan. I mean there he was, a little fever, but you know, people get fevers all the time, so there was no reason to stay at home. And I only had a few things to shop for at the store. I was going to make him some soup, and when I returned he was gone except for the bloodstains, naturally . . . And then the police . . . It seems like only the other day that I first met him—oh, I know this doesn't interest you, but do you mind if I continue just a bit?"

I nodded to show that she should go ahead. I'd always liked Gertrude, but this was the longest conversation we'd ever had.

"I was just out of college, with a degree in art history, and was at a party where everyone wore masks. Claude was a pirate; I forget now which one, Blackbeard or Redbeard—one of those colors—and he looked so dashing I couldn't believe it when he told me he was a small-business owner. I guess that was when I fell in love." She paused. "And now he's gone."

As if a dam had burst, she began to sob out loud for the first time that evening. "I'm so afraid . . . Suppose whoever did that to him comes back . . . You don't know . . . I can't even begin to say . . . Claude . . . he . . . I asked him . . ."

"Asked him what?" I asked.

Between her sobs and a certain slurring quality that the medication produced in her speech, it was hard to tell exactly what she meant but, filling in her ellipses, I surmised that Spinner's tale might well have involved gambling debts, a fondness for recreational drugs, and several bad investments in high-tech stocks. She said she'd asked him to be more prudent in the future. I looked at her. The corners of her mouth had sweet, tiny wrinkles. "Don't worry," I said. "I'm sure everything will turn out to be fine."

She nodded like a little girl.

Gertrude let several seconds pass. "I keep seeing Claude the way he was this morning when I left him sleeping. His eyes were shut and he was breathing through his mouth the way he always did. He looked peaceful, even though his nose was running." She straightened her skirt and looked at a poster of a passenger pigeon I had stuck in a little alcove near the door. "Thank you, Jonathan," she said. "What kind of bird is that? I don't believe I've ever seen one." Then, without waiting for my answer, she continued. "Right now Mister Twisty's is all I really have left of my husband. I don't know your plans, but at least until things are finalized with Claude's life insurance and everything, I'd like to ask if you'll consider continuing to work there. I know Claude was your boss, but you know the business as well as he does. I mean, he did. I'll make you manager."

"Don't worry," I said. "I'll be there if you need me."

"Thank goodness," she answered. "I don't know what else to do. In that case would you mind going in this morning to open up? I'll give you the keys."

I reminded her that I already had them.

"Thanks." She began to cry again.

I patted her back, at a stupid loss for words. "Hang on. Spinner would want us to get through this. I'm sure of it."

"Thank you, Jonathan, " she repeated. "Thank you so very much."

"You're welcome," I said, and called another cab to take her home.

The next morning at ten, when I arrived at Mister Twisty's, there was already a line at the door. No doubt many people had been drawn there by the news of the crime, but a substantial number simply wanted their midmorning yogurt-wheat germ shakes, an experiment begun by Spinner that had been growing in popularity over the past few months. I took down the caution tape from the night before and went inside, a trail of customers following behind.

In the weeks that followed I ran the store while Gertrude mostly stayed away, except that every day at exactly four in the afternoon she arrived carrying a fresh-baked pie. One day it would be cherry, the next rhubarb, or boysenberry, or lemon meringue, or pumpkin, and so on. I assumed that this baking business was part of some private healing ritual and that it would end when she was ready. So each day I would cut myself a slice and add what was left to the day's offerings; they proved extremely popular. Meanwhile, I thought about whether I should tell Gertrude about the women in the basement. In the first place, there never seemed to be a really good time to break the news; and in the second, there was the question of who was to blame. It was true that if the women were discovered it would be hard to prove to the police that Gertrude hadn't known about them. On the other hand, if she *had* been ignorant and I were the one to tell her, in her eyes I would be Spinner's accomplice and guilty of withholding information. If that were the case, she might well call the police and tell them that, unbeknownst to her, she had put a monster on the payroll.

But the bottom line was that the women in the basement remained, and I had to keep them alive or I would be a murderer. After a couple of near disasters with the pumps and the like, I learned to maintain and repair the apparatus that sustained them, and the flow of old guys in and out of the basement continued. I thought about changing the lock—whatever deal the club had with Spinner surely had been canceled by his dying—but if I did that, what would prevent one of them from phoning in an anonymous tip to the police for revenge? What else did these old men have in their lives, anyway, and, besides, it was hard to see how they were doing any harm. On the contrary, following their visits, I always found a crisp one-hundred-dollar bill on the small table in the center of all those cylinders. So I swallowed my first impulse and did what I had to do: I put down a couple of throw rugs to brighten up the place and added a vase of dried flowers. It looked nice.

"Those men," Gertrude asked me one Sunday afternoon after six or eight of the old gentlemen had made their way down the stairs into the basement, "what do they do down there? Claude said they have some kind of a club. Is it like the Kiwanis, or Rotary?"

"Sort of," I said. "They don't cause any trouble and they even pay a little rent." I thought for a moment. "A hundred dollars a month, I believe it is. I'll mark it with the receipts." Gertrude shrugged, and that was that, for the time at least.

Which is not to say I didn't think about the men who had murdered Spinner. Had they found what they wanted and then killed him, or killed him because they hadn't? Was the murder even related to those girls down in the basement? Probably, but possibly not. Could it be that Gertrude's sobbed-out suggestions about gambling debts were correct? Could Spinner have been seeing another woman, and had her jealous husband sent the two men who came for him? Could one of them have been the husband himself? The human heart is a strange thing, and though I hated to pass judgment, it was hard not to wonder. But unlike the cops on television shows, the real ones who were investigating this particular crime never got back to me at all.

Business at Mister Twisty's, far from dropping off in the aftermath of the crime, became better than ever. Gertrude gave me a raise, and with the extra money I'd already gotten from the old guys (minus operating costs and so on) I bought myself a chess computer. For the first time in my life, except for the matter of the girls, things seemed to be working out.

After a surprisingly long time (several weeks, actually) the coroner finally expelled what was left of Spinner from the morgue's sluggish digestive tract, and we buried him on a sunny Thursday afternoon. The only mourners in attendance were a few of the merchants from the Mall Merchants Association, of which Spinner had been a charter member. Gertrude had baked a ton of banana bread, and far less than half of it got eaten. Steve, from Pets Incorporated, addressed Gertrude and the rest of us standing at the graveside. "You were married to a strange guy—no offense, Trudy—but when it came to matters regarding the mall, he was the size of Mister Twisty himself."

Gertrude took the memorial service pretty well. "Do you think Steve is attractive?" she asked the following day. "He smells a lot like pet shop, if you know what I mean, but still he seems quite nice."

I told her I hadn't thought about it, and over the next week I ate a lot of banana bread, which turned out to keep quite well in the freezer. Since Spinner's death, Mister Twisty's had turned into something like a historical landmark, and his memorial service seemed to solidify that status. People came, licked their cones, and left. On Sundays the old guys trickled in and trickled out. The health inspector, Bernie, came and went. Gertrude brought her pies by every afternoon, and on Fridays she stayed longer and went over the accounts. Steve began to pay more visits when Gertrude was around and then, much to my relief, sort of faded away. For the first time it occurred to me that if Gertrude remarried I might be in trouble, but she seemed happier and looked healthier than she ever had when Spinner was alive.

"If you don't mind my asking," I asked her one day, "how are you getting along without Spinner? You seem a lot better than you did when you first got the news."

"Oh Jonathan, thanks," she smiled. "If there's anything I believe in, it's giving mourning a chance to be itself; and luckily, I've found a wonderful support group. It's called Spouses Without Spouses, and we do a lot of walking around and spiritual meditation. The name has a certain ring to it, don't you think? Anyway, don't worry, I'm doing fine."

She gave me a wink.

I didn't know whether to be glad or to worry.

I spent my time behind the store's cheerful coral-colored Formica counter, wearing my white and red paper hat, cleverly designed to look like the same one Mister Twisty sported as he skied down our roof. For most of the people who came in and out of the shop each day, I grew to embody Mister Twisty himself, while Gertrude was only a pale, flitting presence, and Spinner, when he was talked about at all, slipped quickly into the realm of some sort of semi-mythic figure. I smiled, gave extra sprinkles, and then swept them off the floor; I wiped away the sticky fingerprints and refilled the napkin dispensers. But as good as things were, one problem remained. I began to make it my habit to stay behind after work every night for an hour or two in order to pace around the basement, watch the girls, and hope to discover an answer to their current unhappy state. Nothing was forthcoming.

During those hours I inevitably found myself standing in front of the woman I called Mary Katherine. Apparently, whatever attraction the original Mary Katherine had had for me was still working. She made me feel like a creep but I couldn't stop looking. This woman's—Mary Katherine or whoever she was—toes were short and chubby: toddler toes, optimistic toes, touchingly decorated with sort of a pink-grapefruit polish, so chipped and worn that she must have applied it several weeks before she had bumped and tripped her way toward the threshold of eternity only to be suspended before actually reaching it.

The woman's arches were high. Had Mary Katherine been a dancer? I thought she might have said something about taking dance lessons, but after all these years I couldn't remember. This woman's feet were short and wide, cheerful and practical; no-nonsense feet. Her ankles were narrow, with the anklebones protruding rather more, I believed, than might be healthy for a dancer. Come to think of it, I had known several for-sure dancers, and their ankles had been particularly sturdy. One night I noticed a slight nick above one of the woman's anklebones (her left). It must have happened when she was shaving, and it struck me that I'd never given the subject of hair all that much thought. I leaned forward. Sure enough, I could just make out a slight stubble, but no more than that, on the surface of the woman's skin.

I was reminded of that ghastly folklore about how hair and nails continue to grow after a person dies. Why *hadn't* the hair of these women continued to grow? Mary Katherine wasn't dead, but perhaps there was something in the acidophilus that inhibited it, something that one day might be marketed as a depilatory. I resolved that once this issue of the women was cleared up, I would look into it. There was big money there, I was certain.

Each night, my examination began with the woman's feet and moved upward. Her shins were as streamlined and smooth as the legs on a Danish Modern coffee table my parents once had. Her knees, friendly and yet fragile, were a symphony of flat and rounded planes, dimples and sinew. How often I had held Mary Katherine's right knee in my left hand while she drove the two of us to the donut shop just a few miles down the road from my dorm, moving my hand only to change the station on the radio of her old Dodge from rock 'n' roll to easy listening and then back again; my other arm resting out the open window, as all the while I looked toward the horizon for my first glimpse of the giant donut sculpture strapped to the shop's roof that would signal our destination, and which, come to think of it, seemed a premonition of the life that awaited us, although in different ways, at Mister Twisty's.

Leaving her knees, my gaze continued its nightly ascent, as if my eyes were temporarily mounted on one of those machines they use for changing streetlights—cherry pickers, I think they are called. Above her knees were the slightly flattened sides of her thighs—the woman could stand to eat a little more if she ever came back to life—tender and white and oh-how-soft they were, like golden whipped cream or, better, like the muzzle of a friendly horse. Up, up, up the cherry picker on which my eyes were riding would attempt to struggle, approaching, but not quite reaching, that actual cleft, the source of life, though not, alas, for her. Up, up, and up. But no matter how many times I tried to gaze with the frank intimacy of a lover at that particular part of this woman who, I imagined, was Mary Katherine, my eyes seemed unable to reach that actual tender, and to me (despite the fact I knew it was bathed in a cool mixture of yogurt), smoldering spot I had once gazed on with such pleasure. Was guilt the reason the cherry picker's gears began to scream in protest each time I attempted to use its simplified controls to raise its little basket that contained my vision beyond a certain height?

"Rub-a-Dub," I would say, and tap the glass, but there was never any answer.

6

It was a morning in October, just as I was about to leave for work at Mister Twisty's, when I took a moment to observe Captain Bloxheim out in front of the apartment complex, watering his spot of grass, as usual, and it occurred to me that maybe it wasn't the grass at all he was interested in, but water. I watched him as he moved the hose from left to right and back again. Every once in a while he lifted his end of it and let it fall, creating a sort of parabola. Here was a man, I thought, who has seen suffering, and grief, and better days, too; but while he may have been discouraged from time to time, clearly *he* had not let himself be overcome by bad luck as I had. He had not lost his pleasure in the small things of life. At any rate, since I had last seen him he had recovered whatever good grooming habits he had let slide; now he was out of his bathrobe and wearing a Hawaiian shirt with a pair of smart dark-blue slacks.

A woman pushing a baby carriage full of groceries came by, and he directed his stream to one side to let her pass. A kid wearing a red backpack went by on his way to school, and the captain kept the hose where it was. I walked outside. "Good morning," I said.

"Good morning to you, Jonathan," he said. He resumed moving the hose right and left, and then shifted it to a pine tree that was losing most of its needles. "If you don't mind my saying so, you look like a man grappling with an unbelievably difficult problem."

"Me?" I said. "Maybe, but who isn't?"

The captain looked more deeply into my eyes and rubbed his narrow moustache. Though it was still early in the day, he had already shaved, and if I wasn't mistaken I caught a whiff of Old Spice. His gray hair was covered by his naval officer's cap. "Actually, plenty," he answered. "But the fact is that your problem seems to be of a greater magnitude than most people's. I've seen many an able-bodied seaman and mate go mad during my years at sea, so I'm pretty good at reading faces. Your trouble, if I can hazard a guess, has to do with love. Forgive me if I'm overstepping my boundaries, Jonathan."

I was about to say he had, but then I thought about it. This ancient sailor, in about thirty seconds, had hit the marlinspike squarely on the head. Love, I thought to myself. Where had it all begun? With Mary Katherine, certainly; but then most completely, and I would have to say tragically, a year later, with Elberta.

We both stood there for a minute. The water ran onto the sidewalk.

Elberta's hair was red as the inside of a watermelon in August, and her eyes were as blue as antifreeze. She had a wide mouth; fierce, thick eyebrows; and an attractive scar on her lip that she had gotten, she said, in a mix-up with a hay baler. She'd been raised on a farm in the Midwest and, like me, was alone in the world. She was everything I wanted in my rebound from Mary Katherine, but what Elberta saw in me I couldn't guess.

I refocused. Across the street a mailman made his rounds, a heavy sack banging against his thigh. Captain Bloxheim moved his hose from the pine tree to a patch of ivy that was brown around the edges.

Elberta and I had met while we were still in college, and like most young people we would sit around every morning reading poetry out loud and drinking black coffee. In the afternoons we went to a few classes, and then evenings jumped into bed and made love. In short, my life with Elberta was practically ideal, except for one small thing: no matter what experience the two of us shared—sex, food, poetry, music, a sunset—Elberta, in every case, seemed to experience it more deeply than I did. She and I might be out driving in the country when Elberta would spot a sign that announced, "Scenic Vista." "Look!" she'd shout at me and pull off the road (something I never would have done on my own, even if I had learned to drive), and then, when I finished staring before she did, she'd give me a look as if to say, "How could you be such a boor?" In time, of course, I learned to keep my eyes focused on some spot in the distance until she was ready to leave. Then, if I could quickly toss in, "Wasn't that amazing?" she seemed satisfied.

I watched as the mailman walked from house to house, and with each delivery his load lessened. The opposite of my life, I thought.

So there we were one morning, reading the poetry of Walt Whitman, Elberta enjoying it more than I was, when my old friend Carl came up the walk.

"Hey, you two," Carl said and sat down next to us. He grabbed the poetry book and read a few lines. "Wow!" he said, and closed it. Elberta looked at him appreciatively.

Then Carl said, "I'm going on a quick trip to Mexico, and I wondered if you wanted to come along for company."

"Mexico?" I said. "Right away?"

"Sure," he answered. "It will only take a week; nobody will even know you're gone." Carl had a yellow VW bus with a mattress in the back and was always going places—some said to buy drugs, but I never really knew. I looked at Carl. There was a time when he had dated Elberta, but despite the fact that he was in great shape and worked out regularly, Elberta had broken off their relationship. Once, I pulled him aside to ask what, if anything, had gone wrong. He said he didn't want to talk about it. "I'm *your* friend now," he said.

I looked over at Elberta. She was sitting cross-legged, wearing only a short, nearly transparent blouse and her white cotton underpants. "What do you say?" I asked her. An hour later we were driving south to the border, passing around a joint and singing along to the music on the radio.

I watched the captain, with his hose, his dapper moustache, his gray hair, and his just-beginning-to-stoop posture. I wondered whether he had any memories similar to mine. His hose wavered, as if to nod in reply. In one corner of the ivy I could see a dead rat, wet from the hose.

That first day we crossed the border without any problem, and by evening we were driving down the hot, dry roads of

Mexico, looking out for donkeys and cattle and stray dogs, all of which seemed to think the highway had been built for them alone, when we saw a man standing in the distance, his thumb stuck out for a lift. Carl slowed the VW down and motioned for me to slide the side door open.

The stranger was young, about sixteen was my guess, and he looked like a deer, with smooth brown skin and large dark eyes. Something, however, perhaps his clothes, which were of a different cut from those one ordinarily saw in Mexico, made me doubt that he was a native of that country.

"How far do you want to go?" Carl asked him, and the stranger replied in a language that, while none of us actually knew Spanish, didn't sound a bit like Spanish. He gestured with his finger to indicate the direction we were heading. Then, surprisingly, even though the front seat next to Carl was completely vacant, the stranger ignored that, stretched out on the mattress in back with Elberta and me, and immediately fell asleep. Soon, probably as a result of the combination of a warm day and the movement of the van, Elberta fell asleep, and so did I.

The captain had moved his hose away from the ivy and onto a patch of dirt, which the water was having trouble soaking into, and a small puddle, maybe an inch or so deep, had started to form, spreading toward my feet.

But after a while—I don't know how long exactly—I woke, and seeing that Elberta and the guy were still knocked out, I moved up to the front to sit beside Carl. Carl kept driving the VW bus south, dodging dogs and cars and cattle, and I kept him company by fooling with the radio, which only had Mexican music. I don't know how long this went on, but after a particularly loud trumpet outburst, I glanced in back to see whether either of the sleepers was awake, and what I saw was Elberta and the guy, still asleep, and holding each other like two kittens, or children—touching each other just because they were there. Part of Elberta's shirt had become untucked, and I have to admit, though it was sweet, I was bothered a bit, not so much by what they were doing (because really they weren't doing anything) but by the thought that maybe Carl would see it, or already had, and begin to get ideas of his own. I kept quiet, turned up the radio, hoping to wake them, and looked out the window at the dust and the shacks and the cacti.

Maybe the radio business worked, because soon Elberta yawned and so did the stranger. It was beginning to smell a lot like Mexico at that point—charcoal and chilies and heat—and I could see that Elberta was starting to get excited in the way she always did, poking her head out the window and bouncing on the mattress like a kid. "Now smell this. Now look at that," she kept saying, and the stranger, or guy, or whatever he was, started doing exactly that, and pretty soon he was bouncing right along with her on the mattress, and the VW bus started to fill with the smell of their sweat—hers, which I knew, fragrant and like the scent of water in the middle of the desert, and his, pungent and nutty.

The puddle from the Captain's hose was getting deeper, and part of it was touching the edge of my shoe. I should move, I thought, and yet such was the force of my recollection that it had paralyzed me.

Elberta spotted some ridge in the distance, and she shouted for Carl and me to look because it was so fantastic—shaped like a boat or something, and so Carl and I looked, and it *was* shaped like a boat but then so were a lot of ridges, and nonetheless I was about to say that it was amazing, as I usually did, but the stranger began pointing and laughing because he was as excited as she was, and he wasn't faking it the way I did, and then the two of them were pointing and laughing, and I could see Elberta's face was all lit up as it got sometimes during sex; so that was when I first began to think that there might be something going on I didn't entirely care for.

This continued for several hours. Elberta would get excited, and so would the stranger, and after a while Carl and I were just sitting there in the front of the VW bus, giving each other these looks as if we'd been left out of that particular movie, and then the two of them would settle down again until one of them started pointing at something else, some item of the landscape, and then the other would join in, and they'd both get excited all over again.

Eventually, it came time for us to camp for the night, so we pulled off the highway, and I shook the guy's hand to indicate that it was the end of the road for him, and Carl did too—I was trying to be "laid-back," you know—but Elberta hung on to his arm and said we couldn't possibly send a stranger on his way in the middle of the night without food or anything, and who knew what sort of bad people were out there, because she'd heard stories of bandits in the hills who preyed on strangers, and the best thing would be for him to spend the night there with us. Well, she was making sense, and I didn't want to look like a jerk in front of the woman I loved, so I agreed.

I studied Captain Bloxheim as he took a sip from the hose and wiped his mouth. I didn't know how he had acquired his patience—perhaps through his long years of standing watch—but he seemed not at all surprised to see me standing there and saying nothing.

We pitched a tent and made a small supper, which we offered to the guy, who, after first making gestures like, no, he couldn't possibly, wound up eating a whole lot, mostly because first Elberta would take a bite of something, maybe to show him that it was OK, so he'd try it out, and then she'd offer him a bite, and another, and so on; and the whole time the two of them were giggling like kids, acting as if Carl and I weren't even there.

"Relax," Carl said. "He'll be gone in the morning." Then it was dark and Elberta and I crawled into the bus to sleep while Carl took the tent. The stranger, whose name we still didn't know, stayed outside, making motions as if he wouldn't dream of disturbing Carl's space.

About three or four in the morning I woke up feeling cold, but when I turned to Elberta to pull her close to me, I realized that she wasn't there. She was lying outside, holding the stranger, who didn't even have a blanket to cover him, and they were both asleep. I stared at them for a while, to make sure they weren't just pretending to sleep but were really kissing or screwing; but they weren't, so I went back inside the bus, where at least I was out of the wind, and after a long time fell back asleep.

The next morning Carl poked me and pointed outside the bus to where Elberta and this guy were still sleeping. So I made a lot of noise and they got up. The funny thing was that Elberta didn't apologize or offer any explanation. She didn't say anything at all about where she had spent the night, but instead kept on pointing and laughing with this stranger, who in turn kept on pointing and laughing with Elberta. I was starting to get annoyed, but it wasn't until they started feeding each other breakfast that Carl pulled me aside.

"I don't mean to interfere, but do you want me to handle this?" Carl asked.

"Hang on," I answered. "This is tricky, because I want to respect Elberta's space. Don't forget that you're not the one who's with her now."

"I still think we should teach him a lesson," Carl said. "And the sooner the better."

The day in St. Nils was getting warmer. The water from the hose was getting deeper, and the soles of my shoes were getting wet. Still, there was something that would not let me move. Once the Play button of my memory had been pushed I seemed unable to find the button to turn it off, or even to put it on pause.

We finished breakfast, but when it came time to say good-bye to our passenger, Elberta pointed out—I had to admit quite correctly—that it was stupid to leave him behind when we were all going in the same direction; and because I still couldn't bring myself to tell her that I was jealous, which of course I was, I had to agree with her. Carl gave me a look, though, as if to say, "Don't worry," so we all got back in the van and headed farther south.

But that morning things were worse than the night before. By then Elberta and the stranger didn't even make a pretext of being separate, but instead sat in the back in some kind of mutual reverie, staring into each other's eyes, holding each other on the mattress. The one time I went back to talk to her,

Elberta gave me a glance, and they both started giggling. Carl was right. I had to do something, and fast. But what?

Finally it was when Carl stopped for gas at one of those hot and dusty shacks with only a cooler of soft drinks and a few stale sugar cookies for sale, that I got my idea. We had paid for the gas, Carl and I, and Elberta had gone to use the restroom, or what passed for one. The stranger had trailed after her, like he was going to use it when she was done, or keep guard. Or maybe they planned to start necking the minute they got out of our sight.

"What a place," Carl said, shaking his head. He was right. There was nothing around for miles but dirt and cacti.

And then I thought of something: suppose we left the two of them alone there for a while just to show Elberta that if she liked this guy so much, maybe she should see how well she would do in the middle of nowhere with no transportation or money, without me, but with only her precious stranger. Neither of them, as far as I knew, could speak Spanish. It would be an important lesson about what a scary place the world is. Carl and I would drive off and hide for an hour or two, and then, when Elberta was getting really panicked and finally started regretting having treated me that way, Carl and I would come back. I'd be a hero and Elberta would be all over me with gratitude. At that point I figured we would leave the stranger with a little of our food and even a couple of bucks. After that, Elberta and Carl and I would continue on our trip with everything back to the way that it should be, maybe even better.

So that's exactly what we did. While they were off using the facilities, or whatever they were doing, Carl and I drove back north the way we'd come, until we found a place with shade where we could stop. We pulled off the road, and smoked a joint, and then after about an hour we drove back to find them.

My socks were wet. Were the captain's also? Either he was so absorbed by watering that he couldn't feel his feet, or all those years amid waves and spray had left him used to standing in a certain amount of liquid. Still the story rolled on. I couldn't move.

When we got back to the station, neither Elberta nor the stranger was around. The owner pointed south, and made a gesture with his thumb to show that they had hitchhiked out. Then he pointed to the clock and held up ten fingers. We'd missed them by about ten minutes. "This is even better," I told Carl. "We'll trail after them, and then, when their driver lets them off and they have totally and completely given up all hope, we'll be there to rescue them."

"Perfect," Carl agreed, and we headed south.

Except that we never found them. At first, we drove dead south for hours, expecting to see them at any minute, standing in the shade of the next cactus, sweating and thirsty, or maybe waiting at the next roadside taco stand or gas station. But they never appeared. Then, in a panic, we just started driving around, and for the next week Carl and I covered half of Mexico in an aimless rush. We knew that they could have turned off at any point, and could have been staying in some small village or, for that matter, might have hitched a ride back to the United States, but still we kept driving around, asking everyone if they had seen a man and a beautiful woman hitchhiking together, hoping for a clue, or something, but as many people as we asked, no one had seen them at all.

Eventually, we gave up and headed home. It was the longest and most silent trip I've ever made, and when Carl dropped me off at my apartment, I half expected to see Elberta, laughing because she'd known what I was doing all along and now had taught *me* a lesson. But there wasn't anybody. In the days that followed, with every telephone call, with every knock on the door, I expected to see Elberta, but she never came back. Had she stayed in Mexico with the stranger? Had the two of them been captured by bandits and killed, far from anywhere, buried in a shallow grave, never to be found? Had Elberta eventually left the stranger, tiring of him as she had of me, and found someone even more enthusiastic about the wonders of landscape and poetry than either of us had been? I never knew, and ever since that time, for one reason or another and through no fault of anyone's, a certain something seemed to change in my relationships with women; some confidence that things would turn out right slowly slipped away.

The captain began to move. "I really have to go now," he said, "but in case you're wondering, it's our landlord who pays the water bill."

I returned to my apartment to change into a dry pair of shoes before I walked to Mister Twisty's. I'd be late, I knew, but my mother always used to say that it was never a good idea to stand around all day in shoes or socks that weren't completely dry.

7

I walked through the front door of Mister Twisty's a few minutes past our official opening time, but luckily for me no customers were waiting. Unluckily for me, Gertrude was. She was standing next to a pie on the counter. "I just arrived," she said. "I was thinking I'd drop this apricot-peach off early because I have a Spouses Without Spouses field trip scheduled for this afternoon. It's a baseball game, and though I don't much like baseball, I thought it might take my mind off grief for a little while. When I saw the place was closed, I was worried. One of the things that's happened since Claude's death is that I get really, really worried if somebody is not where they said they'd be. I know it probably doesn't make sense, but apparently it's a fairly common reaction in those who have suffered a loss."

"I'm sorry," I said. "I had an accident on the way to work, and had to go back and change my shoes. It put me behind schedule."

She looked down at my feet as if she would be able to tell the difference between the shoes I was wearing and the ones I'd left behind.

"Don't worry this time," she said, "but consider it a warning. By the way, if that Steve comes by looking for me, tell him I'm not interested." Then she left.

I don't know whether it was the sight of Gertrude standing impatiently alongside her pie, waiting for me (how long would it be before she decided to find out for herself what was in the basement?), or those memories of Elberta, but I was rattled; and more than that as well. For whatever reason, something seemed to shift inside my head. Where previously I had been quiet, slowly, very slowly, an idea began to form. Just suppose, I thought, I could bring these women back to life and then release them into the world? If I could only figure out *how* to do it, then I could take care of the problem *before* Gertrude ever found out. But how exactly was this to be accomplished? Then, almost simultaneously and more worrisome, in a way, another question occurred to me: Exactly how pleased would those suspended women be to wake and find themselves not only *not* the holders of the million-dollar bank accounts that had been promised them, but possibly even more broke than when they started? What would happen to them once they woke? Those contracts Spinner had spoken of had vanished along with him and, unless the women had kept copies, they might not exist at all. Would the women be angry enough to report me to the authorities, even though I'd been their rescuer? That sort of misplaced aggression happened all the time, I knew. And even if I *was* their hero, and there *were* contracts once they were awake, what would they do until the paperwork was processed? I certainly hoped the women had kept copies. I could ask Gertrude to hire one, possibly even two, on a part-time basis at Mister Twisty's, but what about the rest? And if those remaining had to receive some form of social assistance until a paying job turned up, what on earth would they write down on the forms when they got to the part about their previous employment? Whatever the answer (or answers), my head was starting to hurt. I would have to put off those questions for now. First things first, I told myself, and later on maybe the women themselves could help me out.

The minute the front door of Mister Twisty's was locked for the night I went down the stairs, trying not to be distracted by the girls bobbing quietly in their fluid, and in particular by the presence of the dark-skinned woman, whose regal appearance always made me feel so embarrassed that I often found myself turning away, as if *I* were the intruder, trespassing there in some basement kingdom all her own.

Enclosed by the pale liquid that surrounded her, her hands were almost as small as a child's, yet at the same time seemed uncannily powerful. Her eyes were dark as well, and they looked furious to be trapped in this inexplicably powerless, inert physical form. I noticed for the first time that there was a scar low on her belly, as if, despite her age, which I put at about twenty, she might already have given birth through a Caesarean section. For the first time it occurred to me if any of these women were mothers, with their children still home, watching cartoon specials, waiting for their return.

On the table was a hundred-dollar bill—it seemed that the old guys, however uncommunicative they might be, were an honest lot, at least. There was also an increasing amount of trash, I noted—mostly wrappers from stomach tablets and breath mints and toothpicks. They tended to get caught between the cables and the floor, and were hard to get at with a broom. Not for the first time I was glad that Spinner had put up three large no-smoking signs; I guessed I'd have to make a notice forbidding litter as well.

I pocketed the money and headed straight for the cardboard file boxes. Inside them was mostly what I'd imagined: old tax forms, a few yogurt-order record books, and ancient service directives regarding the cooling machinery. There were only two real surprises, but they were interesting. The first was an idea of Spinner's for guacamole yogurt, which sounded delicious, on paper anyway, and I wondered why it had never made it onto the menu. I might try it out, I decided; maybe in a corn tortilla cone. I'd make up a few gallons for samples and see how they went over.

The second was more hopeful. It wasn't the actual answer to bringing the women back, at least not right away, but it *was* the original recipe for the special acidophilus mixture that had kept them alive and free from the ravages of time. Once a batch had started, I had discovered that each cylinder required only a tablespoon of ordinary unflavored yogurt every few weeks to keep it going, but here was the stuff of creation itself, the Big Bang, so to speak, of the universe of Mister Twisty's basement. For a moment I had the wild thought that I might also find the formula Spinner had claimed would bring the women back to life, but there was nothing I could see that fit the bill. Spinner had told me that when the time came, *they*—maybe even the same people who had been responsible for his own death—would arrive and everything would be taken care of. For the first time, however, I wondered if there ever had been a plan to bring these women back to life at all. How much of what Spinner had told me was true, and how much was made up?

Still, I thought, the original formula might provide a clue as to how I could return the women to their normal state. It was a long shot, but I had to start somewhere. I would have to try an experiment. If I could duplicate the suspended-animation business on some lower form of life, then figure out how to unsuspend it, once I got the process down I could repeat it to rescue the women.

———————

Unfortunately any immediate implementation of either my discovery of the original formula or the guacamole yogurt was prevented by an autumn heat wave; business was too good to do anything but take care of it. So it wasn't until more than a week later, on a morning after a cooling front finally arrived and before I opened Mister Twisty's for the day, that I was able to walk through the door of Pets Incorporated.

"Hey," said Steve, "I haven't seen you since the funeral. What's been going on? How's the grieving widow? Is there any chance of you moving into Spinner's shoes? She's a few years older than you, sure, but that's one classy woman. I gave it my best shot, but you know everything is chemistry, and as much as I tried, Gertrude and I just didn't have it."

"Gertrude is feeling really, really sad," I told him. "I don't know, maybe she's as upset in her own way as you are over the two of you not getting together, and that's really the reason I've come, Steve. Working at the store seemed to cheer her up for a while, but lately she's been telling me she's lonely. She's joined a support group, but I'm not sure that's doing the trick.

I told her maybe what she needed was something to take c[a]
of when the support group isn't there—a pet, to be exact. Sh[e]
got a strong maternal instinct, you know, but she's skepti[c]
so I suggested that she might start with something sm[all].
Something like, well . . . mice."

"Mice, huh," Steve said. "I guess I should have thought [of]
that—me of all people, but you know what they say about [the]
shoes of the shoemaker's children." He showed me a ca[ge]
with a dozen mice, climbing, napping, sniffing, and mun[ch]
ing. I picked out six and he rang me up.

"Well, hopefully these will do the trick," Steve sa[id].
"Now Trudy will have lots of company. How is she feel[ing]
otherwise?"

"OK, I guess. She doesn't share that much with me," I t[old]
him, briefly locking eyes with an African Gray on the way o[ut].

I took the mice back to the store and left them downsta[irs]
but that night, in the basement of Mister Twisty's, whil[e I]
whipped up a batch of the original formula of preservati[ve]
I watched them more closely. Some ate, others slept, and s[till]
others scurried around their cage, halfheartedly looking [for]
an escape route. Meanwhile I thought about the probl[em]
the women and I were facing: if the acidophilus bacte[ria]
(bacterium?) had the effect of suspending time's unidir[ec]
tional motion by the imposition of its own randomly direc[ted]
motion, which confused and disarmed time, so to speak, th[ere]
had to be something out there that had the opposite eff[ect]
something that would redirect time's motion, and thus br[ing]
the women back to the life they so richly deserved.

Accordingly I asked myself, what was the very mediu[m of]
all life? What medium had the ability to take a lifeless tab[let]

rasa, a random set of chemicals, and combine them into a rich, complex, and sometimes even loveable form? Where had life itself begun, and what composed nearly three-quarters of the human body? Water, of course.

I stared at the mice. I would start by trying to revive them with water, and if that didn't work, I'd think of something else.

One by one, I dropped each small body into a quart jar full of the acidophilus solution, screwed on the cap, and turned it upside down. I covered my ears so as not to hear the scratching of tiny claws against the glass (a sound like none other in the world). Six times I watched a small, pink nose press against the interior of the jar (now here, a second later there), trying to use the last few precious moments of life to escape what must have felt, at the moment, very much like drowning (had those women gone through anything like that?), but which, if my experiment was successful, would only be a little nap. Then I listened to the ever-so-slight rocking of the jar itself on top of the wooden surface of the table. Six times that night, I'm ashamed to say, this nightmare was repeated, and six times I fished out a limp slippery pouch, temporarily spent of motion, and six times placed it in a glass baking dish I'd borrowed from Gertrude, and rinsed it under the faucet. To half the mice I added a pinch of salt, and to the other half none.

However, the mice refused to move. Having tasted what turned out to be not a nap at all, they held on to it with all their might. They were dead, dead, dead, and I went to sleep that night horribly discouraged.

But the nature of scientific discovery is a thing unto itself. The very next day I was standing behind the counter of Mister

Twisty's and thinking about what had gone wrong the previous night. I was alone except for a junior-high soccer player still wearing her muddy uniform, complete with cleats and shin guards, and I was right in the middle of making her a Vanilla Swirl when the answer came to me in a flash. What was the source of life itself, I had asked, but when I answered "water," I had overlooked one very important thing.

Yogurt poured over the sides of the cone and onto the floor and might even have filled the entire space of Mister Twisty's if the girl hadn't yelled, "Hey Mister, wake up!"

"Here," I said. "This one's on me."

The answer, of course, was seminal fluid, whose very name was rooted in seeds, or a place for training priests.

Later that same afternoon, when business quieted before the dinner hour, I hung a sign that read "Be Back in Five" on the door and hurried down to Pets Incorporated. I told Steve that the mice seemed to have caught a mysterious virus and died. "But Trudy loved those little mice, Steve, and they seemed to make a real difference for the brief time she had them," I said. "She says she's willing to try again because she believes love is like that, though as far as the two of you go, I honestly don't think she's ready to make any big moves for a while."

"I understand," Steve said. "Who should know more about disappointment than someone in the pet business, where being responsible for the care of so many living things is to get used to tossing out a certain number of dead bodies (though mostly fish) on a daily basis? But Jonathan, I'm clean out of mice at this very minute; some kids just came in and bought the last of them to feed to their snakes. How about something a little less fragile?" He pointed out a good-sized rat with black fur except for a streak of white, which ran up over his skull and ended above his left eye, like a wave. I was about to say no, that he was a little larger than I wanted, but then I thought about it. A larger animal might better approximate the effect of the fluid on an actual human being.

"Well," I said.

"This fellow's getting up in years. I'll make you a deal."

"All right," I told him.

Steve knocked thirty-five percent off the price. "Give Trudy my best," he said, "and be sure to let her know it's OK."

I kept Steve Junior, as I named my new pet, in the basement with the women. On the Internet I found a lab in Cleveland that specialized in rat sperm (what was going on in the scientific world—or in Cleveland, for that matter?), so I sent away for a pint of the stuff. I'd need at least that much, I guessed, to bring him back, but I didn't want to order so much as to raise anyone's suspicions.

Sometimes, while I awaited the arrival of the necessary fluid from Cleveland, I found myself stroking his fur and holding regular conversations with Steve Junior, almost as if he were an ordinary pet, a cat, or even Sparkles. "How are you feeling today, Steve Junior?" I would ask, not really expecting an answer. But then, to my surprise, he'd look straight into my eyes and twitch his whiskers as if to say, "Not bad, thanks, but you should not be asking me, Jonathan; you should be thinking really hard about what you are going to do about this roomful of women down here. They're starting to creep me out."

To which I would reply, "Steve Junior, lay off me for the moment, would you? I'm working on it."

In any case, the old men didn't seem to mind having a rat down there for company, because the hundred-dollar bills kept coming. A few times I found pieces of fresh apple in Steve Junior's cage. At least one of the seniors must have been bringing him treats.

At last the parcel, wrapped in dry ice, arrived from Cleveland, and it was time for the big test. Gertrude was off on some group excursion with Spouses Without Spouses, but every so often she would call to check on how things were going at Mister Twisty's. Was she taking more of an interest in the business? If so, it was a bad sign. Sooner or later she'd take an interest in the old guys' club as well.

After work I took Steve Junior from his cage. I let him look around, but not too long; I didn't want him to get any ideas. Then I rubbed my finger lightly on the base of his neck, a thing he seemed especially to like. He shut his eyes halfway. "Good-bye, my friend," I said. "Be brave. It's just a short sleep, and who knows, maybe I'll see you again on the other side."

I stuffed him into a quart jar full of the yogurt solution, turned it over, stopped my ears, and shut my eyes. Steve Junior was bigger than the mice, so the sounds he made were a lot louder and lasted a very long time. Sometime after Spinner died I had bought a small used refrigerator at the Treasure Chest and installed it in the basement—I can't even remember why now, but it seemed a good idea. When Steve Junior had finished doing what he had to do, I put the jar inside and shut the door. I would leave Steve Junior there, I decided, for a few days, in order to be certain that the test was a fair one and because I did not want to go through this kind of trauma ever again. I reasoned that if it worked on a rat, I'd go straight to a human sperm bank for the women. It was even possible that I could get a discount if I bought several cases of the stuff.

The next few days, frankly, were the worst. When I wasn't working I took long walks (still giving the animal shelter a wide berth, needless to say) and stared at the roads receding into the horizon. What lay where they stopped? Where had they begun? Could anyone ever know? Had my own life taken a fatally wrong turn, or was it only a detour? If so, when had it been? Should I have signed up for French lessons as Mary Katherine had once suggested? Should I have let Carl drive the stranger and Elberta up and down the dusty roads of Mexico while I searched the radio for a good mariachi station? All I was sure of was that, more than ever, I didn't have time to waste. Again I wondered how the rescued women would express their gratitude to me when they woke. But then, on second thought, I decided they didn't need to be grateful at all; I'd be satisfied as long as they didn't have me arrested. For that matter, I realized I had no idea if they would even speak English.

A week passed. It was time for me to bring Steve Junior back into this life.

That night, after closing, I locked the doors of Mister Twisty's, swept the floor, wiped the counters, and headed straight downstairs. I walked quickly to the refrigerator and extracted the chilled container with Steve Junior in it. After laying the glass baking dish on top of the table, I shook out the jar's contents into it: a translucent cylinder of yogurt stuff with a rat in the center.

Bit by bit, beneath the unblinking stares of the women all around me—women who might have been witnessing their own futures—the acidophilus slowly dripped away to reveal Steve Junior's body. Carefully I rinsed his hair, wiped the solution (if only it was!) gently from his whiskers and even his tail. Using a Q-tip, I made sure that his tiny nostrils were clear, so that if and when he did start to breathe, nothing would obstruct them. Once he was perfectly clean, I refilled the jar with the life-giving fluid from Cleveland, pushed Steve Junior back inside, and waited. Time passed, and kept on passing, but absolutely nothing happened.

My experiment was a complete failure.

Slowly, slowly, slowly, slowly, I walked over to the sink with the pathetic container that had contained not only all my hopes but also the hopes (even though they couldn't possibly be hoping them) of all the women in the room, and of Steve Junior, too. I lifted my former friend gently by his tail and laid him carefully on the sink's wooden counter. Empty of life, he had shrunk into a tiny, spent warrior, bedraggled and abused in the name of human science. His mouth was open. His incisors were like two narrow, gray tombstones. The white streak of hair above his eye pointed in my direction like an accusing finger. I felt ashamed. The rat had, in his own way, been as much a pioneer in the epic of human progress as those dogs and chimps they murderously shot into space during the early days of the rocket program, as much a martyr as those rabbits they continue to test cosmetics upon, as much a victim of man's terrible arrogance (and now a victim of mine) as poor, intelligent Buck. But worse than that, he'd been a friend. I rinsed Steve Junior a second time and left him stretched over the drain while the excess water ran off. I would wait a bit, I thought, and then maybe fluff him up with a hair dryer to prepare him for a hero's burial. "Sorry," I told him. "It was not your fault. You tried."

Meanwhile, I got a bottle of Dawn antibacterial dishwashing liquid from the shelf and squirted it into the now-empty jar, which I filled with hot water so I could scrub it out. It was a perfectly good jar, and could always be used for something else. I looked for a brush, found one, and began scrubbing with a fury that reflected my mood. Steve Junior was dead; the women were who-knew-what; and my chances of bringing them back to life were diminishing every day. Plus, every time Gertrude, who trusted me, asked how things were, I felt more and more ungrateful. In my despair I sloshed the soapy contents of the jar directly into the sink, forgetting that I had left Steve Junior's poor dead body lying squarely over the drain. As I turned to put the jar upside down on the shelf to drip dry, out of the corner of my eye I thought I saw something remarkable. I thought I saw Steve Junior give a feeble twitch, although it could easily have been my imagination.

I turned back to the sink.

Nothing.

I gave the rat a poke with my finger and got no response.

It was late, and I was tired and disappointed.

Carrying the jar, I walked back to the corner shelf and left it there.

When I returned to the sink, Steve Junior was gone.

But to *where*, exactly?

And why had he come back to life, only to disappear? Why couldn't he have stuck around so that I could study him? First I had lost Elberta, and now, through no fault of my own, Steve Junior had slipped away as well.

It took a while—much too long, in fact—to realize that, as with all great questions, the answer was really quite simple. Namely, that if the back-and-forth and up-and-down motion of the acidophilus had in effect intercepted and somehow diffused the purely forward motion of time, then the sudden infusion of an antibacterial agent—in this case, the Dawn liquid antibacterial dishwashing detergent—had caused the bacteria's irregular motion to cease and allowed the normal unidirectional motion of time to begin again. In other words, that seminal fluid business was just a wrong turn in the maze I had been traveling toward my quest. Simply put, I had cleansed Steve Junior back to life.

But what had happened after that?

The answer seemed obvious. The frightened rat must have woken feeling betrayed by someone he had trusted and, understandably, terrified by his recent ordeal. He must have looked quickly around, and then, finding one of those cracks that are impossible to see unless you're a rat, dove straight for it and run for his life. I couldn't blame him; I'd have done the same. In fact I had, that day at the shelter.

But paradoxically, instead of the joy I had expected to feel, what I felt instead was fear. Armed with the knowledge I had just been given, I suddenly understood that I was now holding in my hands not just the lives of any number of likeable and human-seeming members of the rodent family, but several real human beings, and with that privilege came as well the awesome possibility that I might fail. I do not know what others would have done under these circumstances, but as for me, I could only feel a combination of nausea and trepidation.

More to the point, what was the difference between a failed experiment and murder in the first degree? And which of those innocent women in the basement of Mister Twisty's was going to go first?

8

In the end, I'm sorry to say, the whole selection process degenerated into little more than a question of who seemed to need rescuing most, and in that regard it was no real contest. I decided that the subject of my first experiment should be the small woman I believe I've described elsewhere as an Eskimo, or Inuit. But who she was exactly was hard to tell because the cylinder that was her home had been pushed into a darkish corner. Also, the fluid she bobbed in—I guessed that she was an early prototype of Spinner's—remained cloudier and more opaque than the others'. No matter what I'd tried to do to improve the situation, her features remained a mysterious blur. In other words, if the acidophilus in which she was suspended was the equivalent of motor oil, clearly she was in need of a change.

The first thing I did was to go to the Treasure Chest and buy a loose-fitting medical smock I could give her to wear when she first revived. It was the kind of garment that I didn't think would be raising anyone's suspicions. After she was back among the breathing, the two of us could shop, possibly by catalog or on the Internet, and she could tell me what sort of outfits she preferred. The next thing was to find a two-day holiday—not an easy job when Mister Twisty's was usually open seven days a week. Finally I chose as my target date Thanksgiving. Thanksgiving was legendary in the yogurt business for its lack of customers (second only to Christmas, though there was a move afoot among some of the larger chains to insert the word *yogurt* into a Christmas carol). So because very few people ever thought of yogurt on Thanksgiving, Mister Twisty's would be closed, and then the day after I could keep it shut if I needed to, because Gertrude would be gone on a holiday hike with Spouses Without Spouses. I would have the place to myself, except for the women, of course. The reason I needed two days was that I had no idea how long the process might take. The Dawn had worked fairly quickly with Steve Junior, but he was of no size at all, and I didn't want to rush it with a real human being. Plus, the Inuit might well need some counseling. (Again, there was that maddening question of whether any of these women spoke English.)

Thanksgiving Day arrived. I unscrewed the top of the woman's cylinder and opened the petcocks at the bottom and, by means of hoses, directed the fluid that had sustained her down the drain in the middle of the basement floor. I had planned, once the fluid had disappeared, to rescue her by leaning a ladder against the side and lifting her out, but what I hadn't counted on was that as the fluid that supported her vanished down the hoses, first her head, then her torso, and finally the rest of her body collapsed under the pull of gravity. All I could do was stand at the top of the empty cylinder and stare down at her small form, almost a child's, slumped in the bottom of her cage like an unreachable thick and furry root at the bottom of a deep vase.

I'm afraid that for a moment I panicked. How was I going to get her out in time to revive her? If I climbed into the cylinder, how would I get myself back up and over its slippery sides? I rushed to the workbench and grabbed a hammer, hoping to shatter the wall that had once preserved, but now threatened, her existence. I struck but, as in a nightmare, the hammer merely bounced off the thick glass again and again. In desperation I picked up the crowbar (a different one) I kept down in the basement and inserted the curved end between the cylinder wall and the metal lip at the bottom, then lifted. With an enormous screech, and finally a crash, the cylinder toppled to the floor, bounced a couple of times, and rolled a few feet away, intact, leaving its former captive within my grasp.

I picked the woman up as quickly as I could. She weighed practically nothing, even dripping wet, but she was slippery as hell, and I carried her with some difficulty to the table I'd set up by the sink. She turned out to be lovely, her skin smoothed by years of what amounted to a full-body facial, her dark hair thick, glossy, and alive, but whether or not this relieved me or made me more nervous, I couldn't say. I rinsed her thoroughly, and when I had finished, wrapped her in two thick white towels I'd bought especially for that purpose. Then I went to work: as she lay there, limp and still wet, I filled a bucket with warm, clean water, added several squirts of Dawn, and swished it around to be sure it mixed evenly. My guess was that another brand might have worked as well, but why risk it?

Removing the towels, I sponged the motionless form beneath me with the detergent solution, beginning with her face and head, then working downward. When the bucket was empty I refilled it, repeating the process one, two, three, four times. With a sickening feeling, I observed absolutely no movement at all. Then, as I was refilling the bucket for the fifth time (I was running out of detergent and kicked myself for not having bought more), I heard what sounded like a moan, or at least a loud exhalation of breath, similar to the sound made by a person blowing across the lip of a glass bottle, but without its usual droll overtones. At that moment, it was a sound from hell itself.

I turned and saw that, although the woman had not seemed to move at all, her eyes, dark and almond-shaped, which had until then remained shut, were now open and staring out into the basement of Mister Twisty's with what could only be called *the most complete and frozen expression of terror I have ever witnessed in my life*, a look that I pray fervently never to see again so long as I live.

Nothing moved, not even her eyes, but the stare deep inside them seemed to arise from an intelligence that was simultaneously aware not only of the monstrousness of the act being perpetrated upon it but also of its own complete helplessness in the matter.

Despite the sound I'd heard, I could detect no motion of her mouth or chest; nor could I detect a heartbeat. I held a mirror that I had thought to bring down to the basement beneath her nostrils and tried desperately to look away from those eyes but could not. They continued their awful stare out into nothing. Nor did the glass show the slightest cloud of breath. And then, thank goodness, as appalling as this may sound, whatever look had been alive inside those eyes flickered once and, like a fish descending to a deeper pool, returned to the place from which it had come. Though her eyes remained open, they were completely empty.

I turned away.

And coward that I was, I left her lying there.

———————————

I ran up the stairs and raced down the street past houses stuffed with happy, healthy, normal families sitting down to their happy, normal, stuffed Thanksgiving turkeys, bowing their grateful heads and giving thanks, passing the relish, the cranberry sauce, the celery stuffed with cream cheese and the olives stuffed with pimientos. I ran past people sitting alone in the all-too-spacious booths of half-empty diners with their holiday turkey specials and their stainless-steel napkin dispensers. I ran past bicyclists and skaters and moviegoers taking advantage of a day off from work. I ran and I ran as if Megamon himself were after me, and when I finally stopped I found that I was back in my own apartment, trembling. I shut my eyes and eventually fell asleep on the couch with a stack of old newspapers for my pillow. There I stayed, mostly asleep, that night and the following day as well (thank God I had no dreams); and each time I woke I smelled the pleasant, fresh aroma of Dawn, saw on my clothing the dried spots of yogurt from carrying the woman across the basement floor, poor thing, toward her futile, frightened, eternal waking into nothingness.

And all the while I lay there on the couch I knew that the woman, whoever she was, lay dead in the basement of Mister

Twisty's. Paralyzed by fear and shame, I knew that I had taken away her one and only chance to return to this life. I had squandered it on a half-baked idea and then had left her there as if she were no more than a discarded box that had once held waffle cones.

I had to do something, but what?

Gertrude phoned to say that her fellow hikers, and she with them, had gotten lost, but that everything was OK, and I shouldn't worry. She sounded excited by the whole experience. She'd be gone a few more days, and she said that I should take care of the store, as usual. I told her not to worry, but instead I hid in my apartment, occasionally walking out onto the balcony and looking over the withered grass and browning ivy and pine tree, which had resumed the dropping of its needles. The place needed water, and I wondered vaguely where the captain was, but I did nothing.

It was only when Steve from Pets Incorporated called to say he'd noticed Mister Twisty's was still closed, and was I all right, and how were things working out with the rat, that I realized that if I didn't go back to the store very soon someone, maybe a fellow mall tenant, might start snooping around and notice that something wasn't right. So where my humanity failed, fear succeeded. The next day I returned, and late, late that night I gently wrapped the remains of what had been the Inuit woman in those same towels I'd used earlier (I couldn't imagine using them for anything else at that point) and waited in the dark until long after the last groups of loitering, loutish teens had disgruntledly, reluctantly gone off to race hot rods or listen to whatever crazy music excited them.

Then, when I was absolutely sure the coast was clear, I picked up for the last time the woman whose life had been entrusted to me, and I carried her, still wrapped in those towels, down to the Dumpster behind Pets Incorporated, where I laid her carefully on top of a pile of empty dog-food sacks. Then I covered her with blocks of Styrofoam, making, in effect, an igloo, and left her there, alone, to await pickup the following day.

And yet, of course, that was not the end of anything. Those eyes and that look haunted me as nothing else has before or since, and the next day, at Mister Twisty's, as I stared out at the mall's asphalt apron, waiting for the sound of the trash truck while the gigantic shadow of Mister Twisty himself lay across the rows of cars and empty parking spaces, an avenging angel, I felt alone and out of place and scared. I vowed that the next time, if there ever were a next time I dared to try such an experiment, I would not fail. I read and reread the daily paper, searching for any mention of a discovered body, and kept the radio tuned to the news station, but heard, thank goodness, nothing.

One morning I ran into Carlos, who lived in the unit below mine with his girlfriend, Jenille. I let him use my carport when he had parties, since I had no car. "Hey," I asked, "what's with the captain? He's falling down on his job."

Carlos blinked a couple of times until he figured out whom I meant. "Oh, the captain," he said. "You mean the guy that does the watering. Jenille says he was feeling poorly—she talks to him, you know—and Thanksgiving Day an ambulance was here to take him to the hospital. I guess he's not back yet. How old do you think he is, anyway?"

I shrugged and Carlos gave a little wave, as if to say, "Life's an uncertain thing, my friend." I had to agree.

One morning soon after that, Gertrude, wearing hiking shorts and sporting a slight tan, stopped into work. She said she'd had a great time with her support group. "What do you think of adding trail mix to our selection of toppings?" she asked.

I told her it was a great idea.

The guacamole yogurt recipe turned out to be a complete failure, and insofar as it had any success at all, it came from people ordering only the cone, which was essentially a tortilla chip with a point on one end.

I needed inspiration, and soon.

9

But instead of inspiration, I sought distraction in a host of empty activities. I joined the Mall Employees' Chorus (I know, but I was desperate), where I learned to sing "The Song of the Volga Boatmen" and "Finiculì, Finiculà." I joined a puzzlers' group, an animal rights group, and a fishing club that offered a cabin by a lake and discounts on night crawlers. If only there had been a branch of the Extinction Club in the neighborhood.

Whenever I returned to the basement, it was the same thing. I held long conversations with the women. I repeated to them the stories my parents used to tell me, leaving out the scary parts. I tried to explain the basics of chess: the Ruy Lopez opening, the English opening, and the Sicilian defense. I sang them songs. I told them the sad histories of the Tasmanian wolf, the Carolina parakeet, the quagga, the speckled cormorant, and the passenger pigeon, and at the end of each one I said, "Don't worry. You'll be fine."

Although the old guys had given no formal indication that they had noticed the missing Inuit, they must have; and from that time on I began to see a change in the way they treated Mister Twisty's. For the first time I noticed fluctuations in the amounts of money they would leave following their meetings. There was no longer the steady stream of hundred-dollar bills, but a couple of twenties, several tens, even piles of soiled singles. Were they coming on hard times, what with increasing age-related medical expenses and all, or were they gently testing the limits? The unspoken rule not to address them directly prevented me from asking. And there were other things as well: after their meetings chairs were not put back, and sometimes, in addition to the litter I had already noted, there were crumpled paper cups tossed around. One Sunday evening after they left I even detected the sweet scent of clove cigarettes.

Gertrude came to Mister Twisty's less and less. Although her pies, when she brought them, remained popular, she seemed too busy to do much baking, and when she did visit, she almost invariably used the back booth as a kind of office to hold meetings with men I couldn't identify. Sometimes they ordered yogurt and sometimes not. For a wild moment I imagined they might be members of the same syndicate that Spinner had once been involved with, but these men, in their plaid sport jackets and tasseled loafers, looked nothing like the picture of gangsters that I carried in my mind, and besides, every so often I thought I could hear light, ungangster-like laughter. Occasionally one of them would pull out a tape measure, walk over to a wall or doorway, write down some figures on a yellow legal pad, then sit back down again. When the two of us were alone in the store, Gertrude seemed distracted, although she was never unpleasant to me in the least. There were times when I prayed that some gigantic event—a war, an earthquake, a fire—might put an end to things, but of course that would have put an end to the women as well.

Then, completely by accident, the women-in-the-basement problem leapfrogged to another dimension. It happened on one of those rare days when Gertrude offered to stay around Mister Twisty's for a few hours because I had to go to the other side of town to pick up a new set of seals for the swirl machine. I missed my bus and arrived late at the supplier's office, only to find that the seals had not arrived. I'd have to wait an hour, the receptionist told me, but they were sure to be in that day's mail. My first inclination was to turn right around and go back to Mister Twisty's, but if I did that, we would be without a working swirl machine, an important part of our business, and sooner or later I'd have to return for the seals anyway. I decided to call Gertrude, tell her I'd be late, and take a walk around the neighborhood to kill some time. After telling Gertrude what had happened I told the receptionist I would be back. Outside were the usual malls, with nail parlors, pizza places, and places that prepared taxes. I thought I recognized one of the donut shops from its short stay in Mister Twisty's mall, but that seemed no reason to pay a visit. It was a warm day, however, and I *was* a little hungry, and it so happened that in one of those malls was the kind of modern franchised yogurt stand that I liked to think Mister Twisty's stood in rich contrast to. Still, I had nothing against anyone who sold yogurt and, as Spinner used to say, it never hurt to check out the competition.

Inside the Polar Palace I looked around. The place was clean, as were most yogurt shops. I thought that I might have heard something about the owner, a yogurt millionaire, from one of our suppliers, but I couldn't remember what. I decided to try something called a Berry Bark Special, a flavor I wasn't familiar with. I waited while the kid behind the counter, his logoed hat and shirt with a cute polar bear holding a cone, finished wiping down the floor in front of a machine. I knew from experience that was where it got stickiest, so I thought I'd let him finish. The kid was tall and his blond hair was a little longer than I believed was good for business, but as an employee, albeit Mister Twisty's only one, what did I know? His name tag read *Kevin*. Some of the scooping equipment and some of the toppings I recognized, and I noticed that we also shared the same linen service.

Kevin continued wiping. "Can I help you?" he said. As he spoke I saw out of the corner of my eye an old guy I hadn't noticed earlier, wearing a porkpie hat and slacks with an elastic waistband, who opened a door off to one side of the counter and shuffled inside. I felt a sinking in my gut.

For the first time ever it occurred to me that all this while I had assumed that Mister Twisty's was the only store with a stash of women in the basement. But suppose I was wrong? After all, what did I really know? Suppose, just for the sake of argument, that every yogurt parlor in the city and throughout the nation had a basement with three to eight women floating in cylinders, visited by who knew how many old guys, how many times a week? How many yogurt parlors *were* there in this country? Given a national average of one parlor for every ten thousand people, I guessed that the total must be thirty thousand, maybe more; and figuring an average of five women per parlor, that came to about a hundred and fifty thousand woman, all suspended inside strange cylinders in machinery-filled basements. And even if only *half* of them had cylinders in them, it would still come to seventy-five thousand, a sizeable number.

I watched Kevin, with his innocuous hat sporting white polar bear's ears, and his bored and impatient look—an ordinary boy, the kind of young man I had been once myself, before Elberta, before Mary Katherine. I shook my head to push away the nightmare that was unfolding: a vision of every yogurt parlor across the land positioned atop cylinders packed with missing women of every race and type. But why stop there? Why only women? What about all the kids who ran away from home to wind up with their faces on missing-children posters? Why not those soldiers supposedly missing in action, or all those old-timers who one day walked out of their extended-care facilities, or the husbands who left to buy a pack of smokes and never returned, or the infants stolen from their cradles, or the toddlers who toddled off in a crowd at the county fair? Why would *they*—whoever they were—considering how ruthless they must be, stop only at women? I realized how naïve I had been. And now, as I was about to kill a few minutes by ordering a Berry Bark Special—whatever that was—they waited, bobbing slightly, their eyes open, staring off into the darkness around them—how many?—as patient as dogs under dinner tables waiting for scraps; all those lost souls waiting to resume their places in life again, to see their families, to make love with their lovers, to do the normal things that people do. And so what if they didn't know what they were missing? Did that make the urgency of releasing them any the less?

Kevin finished his wiping, his face as untroubled and broad and innocent as anyone could wish. "Can I help you?" he asked again. Then he took another look at me. "Are you all right?" he said.

"I'm fine," I told him. I could feel my eye begin to twitch. "I'll take a small Berry Bark Special, if you don't mind."

I turned to look out at the street. It was a perfectly normal scene, with cars traveling and people walking around, doing their errands, everything etched brightly in the burning rays of the sun. No one walking by would ever know there was anything wrong inside. Terribly wrong.

The kid handed me the cone. It wasn't bad, but the "bark" turned out to be some sort of processed seaweed topping and was a little salty.

I got the seals and caught the bus back to Mister Twisty's, where, after I installed them and made sure they were working, I spent the rest of the day brooding about what I'd seen.

That night I had trouble sleeping, so I stayed up watching television and eating popcorn. The foreign-movie channel was showing a work of Soviet-era realism called *Life in My Crappy Little Village*. I was just beginning to nod off, thanks to the bleak black-and-white drama flickering on the screen (a cow is born; a cow dies), when suddenly the scene moved to the outskirts of the village, to a water-boiler factory that had been abandoned as the result of a poorly thought-through five-year plan and generally shoddy workmanship. The bricks of the factory had been carted away long ago by the villagers to make outdoor patios and borders for their gardens, and all that was left was row upon row of the useless water boilers, each about the same size as the cylinders in Mister Twisty's basement, stacked atop one another like bombs on rotting pallets, covered with rust and wind-blown dirt.

I turned off the television, slept, and found myself almost immediately in a dream where, instead of the hundreds of boilers stacked and strewn about the place, there were only two, and their sides were glass. Inside one of them was me, and inside the other was the Inuit.

10

The following morning I got a call from Gertrude. She said she was about to put a couple of pies in the oven. She'd be stopping by later that day to take some pictures of the place, and would be there just as soon as the pies had baked and cooled a bit. She asked whether I needed her to bring me anything. I told her I didn't. The pictures made me nervous, and I wondered what they could be for. But the pies were a good sign. Maybe things were getting back to the way they used to be.

When Gertrude finally arrived, just after lunch, she had her camera, but no pies, and was in a terrible mood. "What happened to the pies?" I asked. "Not that it's any of my business." I wanted to be sure to stay on her good side.

"Oh those," she said. "What a mess. I had them in the refrigerator overnight, and then, when I put them into the oven this morning, I forgot they weren't my usual pie plates, and these had to be at room temperature. The result was they exploded in the oven, and there was glass and filling everywhere. I've been cleaning up my kitchen all morning. Sometimes, Jonathan, I think we should both find other lines of work, and I should just sell this place and move away. At least that's some of the advice I'm getting from my friend Matt, in Spouses Without Spouses. He's a realtor, and he says he has a lot of experience turning over just this kind of property. But I don't know. That's what the camera's for. I'm just trying to get some ideas."

Then, before I could come up with a sound reason she shouldn't sell, at least for a while, the door of Mister Twisty's opened and a tall guy with a nicely trimmed beard, a baseball hat, and a clipboard walked in. It was the familiar form of Bernie, the health inspector.

"Hi, Bernie," I said. "The usual?"

"Sure thing," he answered. "How are you two doing? Good to see you, Trudy. You're looking good these days. I'm sorry to have missed the memorial for Spinner. Somebody said it was really nice."

Gertrude smiled and nodded.

Bernie continued. "Just now I happened to be over at Pets Incorporated buying a case of expensive dog food because my dog won't eat anything else. When I saw you were open, I thought, I'd bet it would be OK with Jonathan if I stopped in and got this inspection over with. It'll only take a minute, because you never have problems anyway."

I'd gotten to know Bernie pretty well since I'd been at Mister Twisty's, so I wasn't unduly alarmed. Yogurt parlors, he'd told me, weren't places that generally gave him much trouble, not like those establishments that use a lot of fat or cooking oil. "Oil," he used to say. "That stuff is like a magnet for vermin, human and animal alike." Bernie's job had turned him, and I guess his dog, too, into a health nut.

While Bernie poked in and out of corners and under shelves, I made him his usual: two scoops of natural peach in a cup, with a layer of shredded wheatgrass on top.

A couple of minutes later he returned. "Well, Jonathan," he said, lowering his voice so Gertrude couldn't hear, "I've got a spot of bad news today, but I promise I'm not going to write you up or anything. Do you see this?" He held out a stiff sheet of white paper with a few brown squiggles that looked like tiny, badly formed potato dumplings. "It looks as if you've got yourself a rat. I'm not too surprised; I noticed you were shut down during Thanksgiving, and sometimes they like to move in when a place is quiet. Good luck catching it. We don't want to upset Trudy, so I won't breathe a word of this, but I'll be back sometime to see how you're coming along with the you-know-what." He winked and, tossing the paper with the droppings into the trash can, he walked out the door, taking his cup of yogurt with him.

Gertrude snapped her photos and left. I filled napkin dispensers, polished stainless steel, and set out cups and spoons. I was in a bad mood myself by then, and to make matters worse, it began to rain, so throughout the rest of the day Mister Twisty's stayed largely empty. When closing time came I locked up and headed back home. No harm had been done, but Bernie's visit had made me realize two things: first, that I needed to stop very soon at McReedy's Hardware and buy some rat traps; and second, that as long as those women remained in the basement, the potential for trouble remained. At any time, Bernie, or someone worse, could find them, and then where would I be? It occurred to me for the first time that Bernie was near retirement age, and I hated to think about dealing with his replacement. And what if Gertrude decided to put the place up for sale? Didn't they have property inspectors and that sort of thing? Once inside, wouldn't the first door they opened after the front door be the one leading to the basement?

However, before I could figure out a way to bring the women back to the world in an orderly fashion, I had to be absolutely sure of what had gone wrong earlier. If I had been a scientist, I could have rented a lab somewhere, pulled on a white coat, gotten a few grants, and sooner or later solved the problem. Even if for some reason the grants fell through, if, say, the peer evaluation boards came back with comments like "Not enough of a track record" or "No clear need presented," I could at least have published a few papers about antibacterial detergent and acidophilus in some scientific journal, monographs hinting at the interesting interaction between the two, and then sat back and waited until someone else came along with the answer. But I wasn't a scientist, and I was fairly certain that if I tried to explain the situation in the basement of Mister Twisty's to a scientific professional, I would only be met with stares of disbelief. All I had to use in this case was my own brain; as far as I knew there was not much precedent for this sort of thing.

Fortunately, there are times in a person's life when sheer brainpower is left in the dust by luck and a little observation. That night, after Mister Twisty's closed and I returned home, I was too tired even to think about cooking, so I went straight to the freezer and found a frozen dinner with a picture of a good-looking meatloaf on the carton. I poured a can of cheddar cheese soup on top to make it taste better and slid the cold dinner into the oven, thinking as I did of Gertrude's visit that day and her mistake in putting a cold glass pie plate into a hot oven. The meatloaf came in a foil tray, so there was no chance of its shattering, but as I shut the oven door I could feel a warm glow from somewhere deep in the back of my head. An idea was forming, and I walked around the kitchen a few times to give it a chance to grow. I began to think that I might know what I'd done wrong in applying the antibacterial agent to the Inuit woman, and it was this: just as Gertrude had made the cold plate shatter by putting it into a hot oven, when I applied the detergent to the woman's body, I had caused a similar reaction. Simply put, I had caused various parts of her to expand too quickly, while other parts couldn't expand fast enough. The poor woman had, in essence, cracked.

I finished my entire dinner and fried up a few eggs besides. My appetite had returned. The trick was to somehow find a way to apply the detergent to every part of the next woman's body at the same instant, yet at that precise moment I could not imagine how to do this. Nonetheless, I crawled into bed confident that by morning my brain would have come up with an answer.

It came to me even sooner than that. What with the meatloaf and the eggs, onto which I'd dumped too much salt, I had been drinking a lot of water, so at about two or three that night I walked to the bathroom and stood there, watching my urine turning a pleasant shade of green in the blue solution of the toilet bowl cleaner (though why they called it "cleaner" I wasn't sure, because I'd never seen it really *clean* anything), the answer struck me. My mistake with the poor Inuit woman had been to put the Dawn directly on her. It had been all right when I splashed it on Steve Junior, because he was smaller, but in the woman's case, her outer layer had begun to thaw before the inner parts. In other words, the next time, instead of removing the fluid and the woman from the cylinder, I should just leave her where she was, climb up to the top and pour *a whole lot* of Dawn straight into the acidophilus. Just how the Dawn would enter her brain I was unsure of—I supposed it would have to be through the ear canals—and then after that, it stood to reason that the reactivated brain would get all the other organs working.

I flushed the toilet. I might waste more detergent that way, but when she came alive maybe I could lower a rope. For that matter, assuming her muscles hadn't grown too weak during all that inactivity, she might even be able to pull herself out of the cylinder on her own.

All that remained was to decide which of the women would be the first to wake from her long sleep.

———————

The next morning, the first thing I did before I opened Mister Twisty's was to go to the door of McReedy's Hardware, my checkbook in hand. McReedy was an old, skinny troublemaker who wore a moth-chewed green cardigan and spent most of his conversations with me complaining about Mister Twisty's customers' discarded Dixie cups and plastic spoons. "I know that disposable utensils are part of Trudy's business strategy, Jonathan," he used to say, "but it wouldn't hurt to impress the concept of neatness on those customers of yours." Still, he was a survivor and, along with Steve, one of the mall's original tenants. If Gertrude made up her mind to sell, he wouldn't have Mister Twisty's to kick around much longer.

As I hoisted a case of giant-sized bottles of Dawn onto the counter, McReedy looked me up and down. "It looks like you've got yourself a real cleaning problem, my friend."

"Yes and no," I said. "You know how it is. Sometimes a person just doesn't want to make a lot of trips back and forth to the store for something as small as a single bottle of antibacterial cleaner, when all he has to do is to walk next door and buy himself a case from a fellow merchant."

"Well," he said, eyeing me, "I suppose that's logical."

I hadn't counted on McReedy being such a snoop. In the future I'd go to a supermarket even though I'd lose out on the twenty-percent discount the mall tenants gave each other. I could wait for a sale, and then fill a shopping cart with the stuff.

"Oh," I added, "you might as well throw in a half dozen rat traps. I've heard that some of the other tenants are having a few problems, so Gertrude told me to stock up, just to be on the safe side. You know women."

McReedy held his front door open for me on my way out, and I lugged the heavy carton of detergent, the sack of traps balanced on top, back to the safety of Mister Twisty's and carried them downstairs.

Once again I looked around the room. Of the women who remained, which would I save from her present state? Or— another way of putting it—whose life would I dare to place in jeopardy?

There each of them was, each deep in whatever dream she was dreaming, like a helpless museum-goer struck by a paralyzing gas that had been pumped into the ventilation system as part of a million-dollar robbery exactly at the same second she was standing there in front of a painting. And what *were* the paintings they were looking at, anyway? Possibly, I thought, they were still lifes, or *natures mortes*, as the French called them. For example, the Asian woman might well have been standing in front of a painting of a vase full of flowers, forever about to wilt, while the gaze of the Latina-looking one might have been focused on a tipped-over goblet and a plate of moldy cheese. For all I knew, Mary Katherine, or whatever her name was, might have been watching a bunch of grapes, each purple globe forever glistening, unable to become raisins, let alone to rot. *Raisins*, I thought, and the eyes of the Inuit woman momentarily flashed before me. At least I *prayed* it was only still lifes of fruit and things that these women were witnessing. They could, I shuddered to think, as easily have frozen in their brains pictures of Porky Pig or ads for suppositories. Or, if somehow they were able to see yours truly, I must have been for them the scary ghost who walked around and checked their fluid levels.

So I studied each of them, the Asian woman, the blonde, the black woman, the Latina, and Mary Katherine, all equal in their silence, their patience, and their innocent incomprehension, and wondered which one I should choose.

All equal, yes. Yet there was something about the Latina, whom I had named Rosita, possessor of smooth olive skin and brownish-black hair that splashed out from her head like a pool of hot cocoa into which a rather large rock had been heaved, that kept me returning. Her eyebrows were stern and full, and her forehead seemed to frown in seriousness.

Her hands were small, but unlike the black woman's, her fingers seemed fragile, and one was bent slightly, as if it had been damaged in a childhood accident, perhaps a fall from a bicycle. Her lips were full and parted slightly. Had she been just about to speak when she was put in her suspended state? Perhaps she'd been about to say to the thugs who put her there, "No, thank you, gracias, I think I'll pass on your kind offer," but already it was too late. I hoped that I'd find out. She was slender but voluptuous, still young, as if just the night before she'd had a dream about becoming a woman, and the next morning, when she woke, she was one.

But there was more: an indefinable extra depth of character buried in Rosita's expression that seemed to take indifference to its limit. It was a look that seemed to say, "Do with me what you will. You, in your petty yogurt-shop world in a small suburban mall, cannot harm me. You, with your endless, insignificant inventories of cones and cups, sprinkles and gummy worms, you cannot begin to approach the innermost recesses of my soul, which shall forever remain a secret to you no matter how much you try to probe them. You . . . mere individual, you . . . you . . . you . . . gringo . . . you shopkeeper. Do what you will. I am beyond you. If things work out, fine. I'll be grateful and I promise not to cause any trouble, but only because it is beneath me. If things don't go quite as you have planned, then, well, you still will not have touched my essence . . . nor will you ever."

I set the rat traps and left.

Never had a day passed more slowly. Around noon Gertrude appeared with another friend whom she didn't introduce. The two of them sat in one of the back booths and laughed about something, then left together. She had not brought a pie. Finally it was time to close Mister Twisty's. Of course I could have slunk off to my airy one-bedroom apartment with its view of the street and returned to the women in the middle of the night, but it somehow felt wrong to leave them even for a few hours when their salvation was so near at hand—and yes, maybe there was the fear as well that I might change my mind. Also, it was a long walk, and I wanted to be as fresh as possible for the job ahead of me. I ordered a pineapple-pepperoni pizza from Luigi's, a few doors down, next to Pets Incorporated, and sat in the booth farthest from the window of the darkened yogurt parlor, watching the headlights of the cars as they entered and left the parking lot. When the last car putt-putted itself out of the last space in the lot and I was sure the mall was deserted, only then did I descend to the basement, where, just to be sure I wouldn't be disturbed, I sat awhile longer, listening for sounds, writing down three different versions of a recipe I had been working on for mock chocolate-chip yogurt, using lentils. Later, when things calmed down, I would have to try all three and compare. Maybe, it occurred to me, if Mister Twisty's closed, I might use the recipe to make my fortune. There were a lot of people interested in a healthier diet these days.

And then it was time to begin.

I looked around the basement once again. Except for the glass of the cylinders, which I tried to keep wiped down, the place was getting dusty for sure; after I brought Rosita back to life I'd have to give everything a real cleaning. Only the chairs, their seats rubbed clean by the trouser bottoms of the old guys who occupied them, seemed relatively dust-free. Mixed in with the money on the table I found four quarters. Was this some kind of message? No matter. There was only one thing I was interested in at that moment, and no one would stop me.

On the stepladder's platform I placed a bottle of Dawn, removing the cap completely so it could pour without impediment. It was my hope that the more rapidly I introduced the detergent and let it spread throughout the cylinder, the less chance that there'd be a repeat of the cracking phenomenon. I didn't want to risk slowing down the operation by trying to squeeze out a large amount by means of only a squirt tip, a process that I knew from experience could tire one's hand quickly. I dragged the silvery stepladder to the side of Rosita's cylinder, climbed up, and unscrewed its top, being careful not to disturb several tubes and hoses that kept the liquid inside circulating.

I reached my hands above my head, ready to pour the Dawn into the cylinder, and stared straight into Rosita's eyes to monitor her progress.

"Hola!" I said. I wanted to say, "Welcome to the world of the living once again. My name is Jonathan, and I will be your guide at least for a while, until you become readjusted to the world," but I didn't know enough Spanish.

Taking a deep breath, I emptied the bottle of Dawn squarely into the center of the tube, right above her head. I was gratified to hear a glug, accompanied by the bottle's growing much lighter, and then another glug, then four more. I threw the spent container into an empty corner of the room and descended the ladder to watch Rosita's dark gaze as the blue-tinted Dawn slowly combined with the pale fluid that had been her place of residence for who knew how long.

Rosita's eyes widened, and her mouth formed a silent O.

I held my breath. I could see a small spasm of life run through her body, and she gave a little shake of her head, as if to say, "Hey, what happened? Where am I? Que pasa?"

I exhaled.

I had succeeded. I pointed to my chest so Rosita would know that I was there to help her out of her present situation and that she should not be frightened by the strange circumstance in which she found herself. I again spoke words of reassurance (even though I wasn't completely sure she would be able to make them out). "Rosita," I repeated, "buenas noches."

I inhaled.

Her head moved again, this time more deliberately, as if she were nodding thanks; and she opened her eyes wide. Rosita took in a deep breath, and then, with an expression of awful surprise, tried to stop inhaling, but could not. Her eyes widened again, her thick eyebrows knit ever so slightly together, and then her body went completely still.

I cannot imagine what it must have been like for this unlucky woman to realize that, after all these years of waiting, what had filled her lungs was not air, but fluid. All I know for certain is that when her eyes widened that second time, she unleashed the briefest, most intense look of contempt I had ever seen on the face of one human being for another. It was a summary of everyone—from every nation and socioeconomic group and every era—who had ever been cheated out of what was rightfully theirs: liberty, life, inheritance, even love. It bored into my own eyes, and then, after it had finished measuring the enormity of what I had taken from her, it measured me as well, and scorned the person who had taken it.

She had deep brown eyes and small, perfect ears.

I exhaled. Using my knuckles I banged on the side of the glass, lightly at first, but then more forcefully.

"Wake up! Hola!"

There was nothing.

"Please—por favor," I whispered, "don't be dead."

Rosita's eyes rolled up so that all I could see were their whites, and one of her knees began to move up to her chest, almost as if she were attempting to climb out on her own, but almost immediately what she was doing had slipped her memory. Then the O of her mouth deflated, and by the time I reclimbed the ladder, reached in, got hold of her, and lifted her out, dripping, onto the floor, she wasn't moving at all.

I tried to save her, of course. I wrapped her in a blanket; I offered the kiss of life, tried CPR—pushing on her chest and doing her breathing for her—all the things that anyone would do in a situation like that, but she must have been too fragile or have inhaled too much fluid for those time-proven methods to work. At least, that's what I tried to tell myself afterward—that Rosita's suffering, as horrible as it may have been, had at least not lasted all that long.

So it was too late. Rosita had gone back into that *nature morte* that I had imagined her viewing, or maybe back into her own nightmare, one in which I was, if not her actual murderer, a nameless and frightening shape born from her subconscious and distorted by the curvature of her cylinder, a thing that had come into her mind unbidden. But unlike the countless other bad dreams she might have had during her confinement, this one had not been chased away.

For a long, long while I could only sit at the basement table, my head in my arms, and weep. Then, thank goodness, I remembered that the following morning was the day scheduled for the truck to come to empty the mall's Dumpsters. Making sure that no one was around (it was the middle of the night by then, so the chances were very slight that I'd be seen), I wrapped her in several large and heavy towels and lifted her still-damp body onto my shoulders and staggered with her up the stairs. Finally, awkwardly but determinedly, I made my way over to the same Dumpster where I had left the Inuit.

When Rosita lay inside at last, I looked around to be sure the alley behind the stores was empty. Then I walked over to the House of Foam, a new arrival to the mall, and pulled three large yellow strips of foam from the Dumpster behind it. I placed one on either side of her, and one on top, like a small, soft, adobe house. One of Rosita's arms was bent, her hand lying lightly across her lips. Gently, as gently as I could, I closed the Dumpster's lid.

"Vaya con Dios," I whispered.

11

It was not long afterward that I saw Captain Bloxheim back at his usual post with the hose. With a heavy heart, I was about to leave my apartment for work at Mister Twisty's when I spotted him, looking the worse for wear: his skin was sallow, and he leaned on a skinny cane with an ivory handle. Possibly in order to get a little sun, he had rolled up the sleeves of his bathrobe, revealing on his thin arms—even at that distance—a tattoo of a palm tree, withered by time and his recent illness until it resembled the plants he was attempting to revive. He moved the hose around frantically, as if to make up for lost watering.

"Captain," I said. "How are you feeling?"

His voice was thin, but determined. "I've been better. Don't ever get old, Jonathan. Look at these plants. They're in terrible shape, and if I can say so, you don't look so great either."

I nodded my head. As usual, the captain was not wrong.

He continued, "You know, when I was in the hospital without much to do, I thought about you sometimes, Jonathan. I know we've spoken from time to time, but the fact is I don't really know a lot about you. So I started thinking as I was lying there: That Jonathan, I wonder how he's doing? How did he get himself in such a mess? Is he from around here? Does he have family? A mother? A father?"

"My father," I said. And as in a theater where a scrim pulls back to reveal a scene behind it, I thought back to the time I said farewell to my father. It had been on a ship, and for the first time it occurred to me that might have been part of my fondness for the captain. The two also had certain physical similarities: good posture and a jutting jawline. In fact, if my father had survived to old age he might have looked much like the captain. But of course, I knew as little about the ex-seafarer as he did about me, except that apparently the bond, whatever it was, was mutual.

"Yes, your father," the captain said. He began to spray leaves off the walk. Meanwhile, I stood there and thought back to the time I had last seen my father.

My parents had been on a vacation, a cruise, and the ship had stopped somewhere warm, the exact name of which escapes me. I was only ten at the time. There were the usual games on board, a lot of food, adults around to supervise the children, and a swimming pool, which was where I spent most of my time. Every so often the ship stopped and everyone left to go shopping. To me one place looked pretty much like the next, but people seemed excited to get off the ship at every port regardless, and then to return to the ship in the evening to discuss their so-called adventures.

Captain Bloxheim finished washing the leaves off the sidewalk and turned his attention to an azalea bush that seemed especially needy. Meanwhile, the memory of that last voyage continued to uncoil in my brain.

During the ship's fourth or fifth such stop I sat in our cabin with my parents, waiting unhappily for them to drag me along on yet another shopping trip. I was wishing that I could just be left at the pool, but apparently there was a policy that no one could go swimming while the ship was docked—possibly to give the lifeguard a little time off, but I never found out why, exactly—when my father let out a strange-sounding groan. At first I thought it was the ship, because sometimes there were sounds like that while the ship was docked, so I looked out a window but saw nothing that might have made the noise.

My mother knew the source of the noise immediately, however. "Robert, what's wrong?" she asked. "Are you feeling all right?"

My father turned to her. "Clarisse," he said, "I seem to have a spot of indigestion this morning. Why don't you take Jonathan out to the shops and cafés along with the other passengers while I stay behind in the cabin? I'm sure I'll feel better soon, and then, when you return, you can tell me about your day."

"Robert," my mother said, "you know I can't leave you behind when you are not feeling at your best. Instead, I propose that we all stay behind, and you try to take a nap. Then later, in an hour or two, when you improve, the three of us can go together on a little shopping tour all our own, without our fellow passengers. Until then, Jonathan can keep busy washing off the shells in his seashell collection, which is starting to smell quite bad, and I can just sit reading this book about local customs and beliefs. Some I find quite laughable."

So my father lay in bed and tossed around until he fell asleep, while I busied myself scrubbing down the shells in my collection. I had found an especially good example of a Striped Fox at the last port we visited, and for me, finding that shell had been really the only reason to go ashore at all. As much as I hated to admit it, my mother had been right; the shells were getting foul, and cleaning them helped a lot. A couple of hours later my father woke up. He looked all right, aside from a fine line of sweat that had appeared along his forehead, and he seemed ready for an adventure.

"I'm feeling better now, my love," he said. He ate a few crêpes and drank a glass of iced tea, without sugar, which was how he liked it. Then the three of us descended the gangplank from the ship, hailed a cab, and drove into town.

The captain staggered slightly to his left but caught himself with his cane. "Don't worry about me," he said. "I'll be fine." I couldn't tell whether he would be fine or not, but I couldn't help being reminded again of that day long ago with my parents.

The town was not large, but the port area was surrounded by many robust, unwithered palm trees, and the streets, dusty and cobbled, were full of bicycles and donkeys—all standard stuff, I thought. As we walked, my mother called to my notice the absence of buildings of more than a single story, a result, she said, of recent seismic activity, while my father reminded both of us, as he always did, that the crafty native population loved nothing more than to fleece unsuspecting tourists by getting them to pay the first price they were quoted. "Never, never give them what they ask," he told us for the thousandth time. "Start low, and then raise your offer only gradually."

Eventually we found ourselves in what was more or less the center of town. We walked from stall to stall, fingered the wares, and nodded graciously at the rising desperation of the vendors, who must have been conscious that, because it was the middle of a very hot afternoon and there were no other customers about, if they failed to sell to us they'd sell nothing at all. I had no idea where the other passengers from the ship had gone, but they certainly weren't anywhere that I could see. We bought a few small things, trinkets to keep as souvenirs or to give away as small gifts when we returned home. In every case we bargained with such vigor, disparaging the quality of their goods with such success that the natives had tears in their eyes by the time we finished. At last we found ourselves standing in front of a small, dark shop. It offered a selection of woolen goods, all of a uniformly poor quality and not remotely the sort of thing a person would want in such warm weather; but then my father let out a groan that sounded very like the one he had let out on the ship earlier that day.

"Take me inside," he told us, as he leaned against the building's flaking stucco exterior. I ran indoors to find the proprietor, who helped my mother half walk and half drag my father inside to the least dirty spot on the floor. There I loosened his tie (my father was a great one for formality) while my mother bent, fanning him with a straw placemat she had purchased earlier.

"Jonathan, I'm cold," my father said, though how anyone could be cold on a day like that I couldn't understand.

"For God's sake," my mother told the shop owner, "bring him a blanket," and she pointed to one nearby, covered with a design of alternating black and yellow stripes, one that even a child like me could tell was of exceptionally poor quality. It was also stained, I could see, in one of its coarse corners.

But instead of moving, the man just stayed right where he was and told my mother, in a not-unpleasant way, "If you wish this one the price will be five hundred U.S. dollars."

"That's ridiculous," my mother replied smartly. "You're trying to take advantage of the situation. In this country a family could live for a year on five hundred dollars. I happen to know that that blanket isn't worth more than twenty dollars, at most." My mother could be forceful, and at that moment I was especially proud of her.

"Nevertheless," the man said, and nodded complacently, "the price remains five hundred dollars."

I touched my father's forehead and could feel the dust stuck to his sweaty skin. I got up and walked over to the corner next to the blanket in question. Up close, it was even shabbier than it had seemed from across the room. It must have been a beginner's work, I thought, perhaps made by someone my own age still early in his career of child labor, or possibly by an ambitious young adult who, having turned out such an obviously unsatisfactory product, had quickly given up his dream of home employment to find a job as a busboy or a waiter instead. Even I could tell now that the proprietor, having obviously stumbled on a customer he thought was in no position to say no, was trying to unload it on our family.

"I'm cold," my father said, a bit more faintly this time, from the center of the stone floor.

"That's completely out of the question," my mother told the shopkeeper. "I'll give you fifty U.S. dollars, and even that's much too high." I knew, of course, that that was far more than the blanket, as shabby as it was, could possibly be worth, and I hoped the man would give in quickly. All I could say in its favor was that the blanket looked warm; if my mother had switched to any other blanket in the shop the price would no doubt have been higher, plus she would have to start negotiations all over again.

"I'm cold." I could barely hear my father. He was starting to slur his words badly at that point but, unbelievably, the proprietor just stood there, waiting for my mother to give in to his price. The man remained pleasant, I must say, but each time my mother raised her offer, he lowered his price only a little, and then repeated, "It's impossible for me to accept less . . . the labor of many hours . . ." and other such completely ridiculous statements.

"Clarisse," my father said, and then he said something else that I couldn't quite make out.

At last my mother had gotten the awful man down to a hundred and ten U.S. dollars when I heard a terrible groan from behind me. I rushed away from the stack of blankets back to my father. We were too late. His hands clenched and unclenched, making small scratches on the filthy floor of the shop, and his mouth opened and closed, as if trying to say, "Jonathan, you've been a good son, and a blanket would have been a real help, but don't worry. I have no hard feelings, and it's too late now anyway. Now you're the man of the family. Take care of your mother and think of me from time to time. Farewell." Then he ceased moving.

The captain, satisfied that he had given the azalea enough fluid to sustain it until the next time, moved on to a privet hedge.

If there was a happy ending, it was that, probably out of guilt, or maybe fear of reprisal from the authorities, the proprietor sold us the blanket for thirty-five dollars. We had a couple of stewards from the ship wrap my father up in it and carry him back to our vessel, from which, a few hours later, we buried him at sea, still in that same blanket.

I listened to the sound of the captain's watering. It was soothing in a way, and I took a deep breath. I could see why he did it.

My mother and I returned home, where Mom married the lawyer who had handled my father's estate. I was sent to boarding school, and then to State College. For one reason or another my mother and I lost touch, although in the beginning I got postcards from her; she and her new husband liked to go on cruises.

The captain stood there watching me, shaking his hose up and down to make the water rise and fall.

"Jonathan," he said, "I may be sick, and I know your job at Mister Twisty's doesn't allow you much time off, but I believe what you need is a sea voyage." I must have made an unusual expression, because he quickly added, "Barring that, I have another piece of advice which I think you will thank me for. I have never spoken much of this, but in all my years at sea I've made the acquaintance of many a ship's cat and parrot, even monkeys and marmosets, without a bad apple in the bunch. If there is anything I believe in, it's the healing power of animals."

I opened my mouth to say something, but he stopped me. "No, Jonathan, I'm not suggesting you buy a pet, although that might not be a bad idea. Why don't you do this: take a trip to the zoo. I visited it myself just before this little bout at the hospital, and I believe you just may find there, as I have so often, exactly what you need." He walked over to the faucet and shut off the water. "Now I'm going inside to take a little nap," he said. "I want you to promise me you'll try it. Let me know how it turns out."

I checked my watch. I was going to be late to work again.

I waved good-bye and walked as briskly as I could to Mister Twisty's. It was tempting to take the short route past the animal shelter, but this was no time to be careless. Despite the sun, the morning was still on the cool side, and with luck Mister Twisty's would be deserted.

It wasn't. When I got there not only Gertrude but also a crowd of people, mostly her age and older, were inside, all wearing the same outfit: black walking shorts and a yellow T-shirt with a picture of a honeybee on the front. They were looking around impatiently, as if they expected something to happen.

"Oh there you are, Jonathan," Gertrude said. "I was just starting to get worried. I've promised all these nice people a free cone, but we can't get the machinery to work. I'd like you to meet some of the members of Spouses Without Spouses. We've just finished an all-night loneliness retreat, and I had what I thought was the good idea to invite everybody here. I'm glad to see you, even if you are late. I was just about to send Matt here"—a genial-looking guy with tanned and hairy forearms gave me a nod—"down to the basement to check the fuses, or whatever. Matt's handy that way, and believe me, he'll be a real catch for someone if he ever decides to stop grieving." She gave the group a wink.

"No need for that," I said, and flipped the master power switch under the counter. "I thought I'd showed you this a long time ago. Remember?" I heard a hum as around me the yogurt dispensers came to life.

Gertrude laughed. "I guess you did, Jonathan, but maybe staying up all night made me forget about it. Forgetfulness is one of the first things that happens when you suffer a severe loss, you know." Behind her several people nodded.

"But forgetfulness is only a part of it," she said. "I'm sure, Jonathan, that you are well acquainted by now with the so-called five stages of grief—denial, anger, bargaining, and the rest—but if not, I won't explain them at this moment." A woman in a broad-brimmed straw hat looked slightly disappointed. Gertrude resumed. "Sometimes it's hard to say whether it's better to forget a loss or just let go of the normal details of daily life in order to do nothing else but face the loss directly; however, I'll be the first to admit it need not be simply one or the other, but a combination of both."

Gertrude paused as several of the people awaiting cups and cones of yogurt appeared to discuss which of the two alternatives they themselves found more congenial. "But Jonathan," and here Gertrude seemed to straighten herself up, "and I'm sorry to have to reprimand you in front of a group of strangers—what is *not* allowed is forgetting to come to work on time. This is the second time it's happened. I don't want you to feel bad, but Matt here has been telling me that he has a younger brother who's been looking for work. He might not be able to do as good a job in some ways as you have, and I have been grateful for how you have held this place together after Claude's death, but Matt tells me Jerome—that's his brother's name—is punctual; and really, if you insist on being unable to arrive when you are expected, this might be a good time for you to begin thinking about a career that better suits your schedule."

"Please, Gertrude," I said. "I completely understand, but I promise it won't happen again." I was humiliated to have to give this speech, but I only needed a little more time to free the women. After that she could fire me or not; it would be up to her.

"Well . . ." Gertrude said, and I could tell that not only I was embarrassed by her outburst, but most of the Spouses Without Spouses were also.

By the time the Spouses Without Spouses had finished their yogurt and left, it was too late to ask what that business of the bees on the T-shirts was about, anyway. *Jerome*—what kind of name was that?

12

That night, as I shut down Mister Twisty's, I looked around. Above me was a ceiling of yellowing acoustic tiles, and below me was a basement full of cylinders of women suspended in yogurt. Behind me was the counter, newly cleaned of smudges, the row of gleaming swirl machines, and the door leading to the basement. In front of me was an empty parking lot. In one corner, near the entrance to the parking lot, an empty pizza box and a greasy pillow that had somehow escaped the House of Foam lay, the two barely touching, like a contented married couple. Oh yes, and several plastic spoons and Dixie cups. So much for people. Animals, I thought, don't leave piles of trash everywhere they go, and they were quiet and serene. Who *wouldn't* want to live with them? It was worth a try. I walked to the corner and found a waiting bus that would drop me at the zoo's main gate.

I had actually avoided the zoo ever since Mary Katherine and I used to go there together; it brought back too many sad memories. Lately, however, rumor had it that the zoo, always struggling to stay afloat, what with the ever-increasing cost of animal feed and competition from televised nature programming, was in trouble. Attendance had fallen, and there had been talk of sending the animals to carnivals and turning the whole area into an industrial park. As a last-ditch effort to save the place, the zoo had hired a public relations firm whose campaign, "The New, Sophisticated Zoo," featured a picture of a camel smoking a cigarette and holding a martini glass (I remembered that in the past the zoo did have a camel, along with a goat, a panther, a raccoon, two snakes, a duck, and several unusual-looking rabbits).

The new zoo, according to this concept, was no longer just a place for weary parents to bring their attention-deficit-disorder-afflicted children to exhaust themselves as they ran from one captive animal to another; nor was it merely an extremely unpleasant but admittedly safe haven, like a refugee camp, for endangered species. The new zoo was now being marketed as a watering hole for sophisticated world travelers who, tired of the usual parade of sex joints, cathedrals, and blues clubs, could stroll among its cages to rekindle the spirit of adventure and the taste for the exotic that had made them want to go out and be travelers in the first place: the desire to rediscover a lost world rapidly being erased by the globalization of commerce and the increasing homogenization of all native cultures.

When I arrived, the evening was already well under way. The arched entrance to the place was bedecked with red and green Christmas lights and blue lanterns. Strolling through the shadows they cast were women in net stockings selling cigarettes, canapés, cans of beer, and simple cocktails served in elegant glasses. Mixed among them were solo violinists and mariachi bands, even, occasionally, a completely nonmusical panhandler. Around me the air was rich with the smells of perfume, tobacco, and roasted popcorn. Perhaps, I thought, this might work after all. Maybe the captain, as improbable as it had seemed at first, was correct, and I might find something inspiring in the presence of so many life-forms different from the ones I was used to. Maybe I would go home, having seen things with a fresh perspective, and release the women, and everything would end happily.

Immediately to my right as I entered was a lone flamingo, its pink plumage darkened to crimson by the colored lights. The shadowed hatchet of its bill, combined with its beady eyes, gave it a criminal look, the kind you might see on a guy caught while stealing car stereos, leaning up against the side of a squad car in his sweatpants and athletic shoes, waiting to be taken down to the station, booked, and then let out on bail. I wasn't sure whether this was a bad sign or a good one.

I strolled along the zoo's dusty and potholed paths, looking for solace in the great book of nature as it spread out before me. I passed a bedraggled coyote, a mask of mange around his eyes; a raccoon, his head resolutely wedged in one corner of his cage; a couple of chickens, each walking in its own tight circle; and the camel I remembered from the past, still there, lying on its knees, its bile-colored eyes underlined by loops of skin that sagged like multiple placards of shame, its hump slumped against a rusting chain-link fence.

The zoo's promotion appeared to be a success. Crowds of jaded onlookers lolled around in evening wear, jostled one another, sipped their cocktails, and made small talk. For a while, I joined a group gathered around a piano player taking requests near the prairie dog condo. All around me people were meeting other people, flirting, breaking off relationships, and exchanging phone numbers. Here, I thought, was life's true purpose: procreation. And maybe once those women in the basement were returned to the world they might like to pay a visit here along with me.

Finally (though the zoo wasn't so large that it took very long) I arrived at the panther's cage. As panthers go, it was a smallish one, and very black. It had a wizened look, and where its fur had been worn away its skin was puckered like the fingertips of a person who has been in water for a long time; except that in this case, of course, the panther was perfectly dry, and even what you might call dusty. The panther stared, not out between the bars of its cage as I'd seen other panthers do, but down at its two front feet, which were buried in bits of Styrofoam and dirty popcorn.

Outside, a small clique of partygoers watched the graceful animal and tried to get its attention. A short, brutal-looking man ran a wet finger around the rim of a crystal cocktail glass to make an earsplitting sound, as his companion, a svelte silver-haired beauty, tossed flamingo-shaped swizzle sticks in its direction. Meanwhile, the panther stared resolutely at its feet as if it were engaged in a contest of wills, and it planned to be the victor.

A teenage hooligan began to bark at it.

The panther's stubborn refusal to look up only made the spectators grow more excited. An old gentleman clattered the tip of his cane back and forth across the cage's bars, and someone set a cocktail napkin on fire. Still the panther's gaze remained pointing steadily downward. Finally, a red-cheeked drunk in tight pants and a leather jacket threw a cup of beer onto the poor animal's muzzle. At last, slowly, painfully, horribly, the panther looked up with an expression that indicated the game had moved outside even the agreed-upon parameters. The slits of its pupils opened for a moment with a look of pure scorn, and then retracted. The crowd was silent. The beer made pathetic rivulets in the animal's fur. From the corner of one of its eyes a drop of liquid ran, and someone in the crowd, a woman, laughed, "It's crying."

Then the animal turned, and I could see that it was staring directly at me. "You," it seemed to say. "You of all people. How can you stand there and do nothing?"

I looked around me. About ten feet to my right was a large rock spattered with excrement from the white-backed vulture. It would only take a second to run over and seize it, return, smash the lock, and release the panther from its humiliation. And sure, the animal would be captured and probably killed in a day or two, but at least for that time it would be able to fulfill its true nature. "Do it," I heard a voice inside me say. Then I thought of Megamon. Had he been happy during his last days at the shelter, or merely irritated? I assessed my fellow zoo-goers once again. It was true they were a fairly vicious lot, but they had not made themselves that way; someone else had done it to them, and if I released the panther, it was likely that several of them, perps and victims at the same time, would be maimed or worse. Then there were the women in the basement waiting for me to free them. Suppose something happened to me along the way that might delay the process?

"I'm sorry, my friend," I mentally signaled back to the unhappy beast. "I have other work I must take care of, others of my own kind I must help first. As much as I hate to say it, I'm afraid you're on your own."

I turned away as the victorious crowd began to jeer at the panther.

The walk home was dark and lonely, but not as long as I thought it would be. As I approached I found the street in front of the building strobing red from the light of a paramedics' van. A small group of people, including the apartment manager, was gathered at the curb. As I walked over to them, a body, completely covered in a pale blue blanket, with a naval officer's cap resting on top, was slowly being wheeled away. Clearly no one was in any big hurry. The emergency, whatever it had been, was long since over, and the paramedics moved like tired stagehands putting away props after the actors had all gone home.

It turned out that the body had been discovered by the apartment manager, who, after seeing the captain's light on, had decided to knock on his door in order to obtain the past several months of rent the captain owed him. Receiving no answer, he peeked in a window and noticed a foot sticking out from beneath the kitchen table. "At first I thought he was just taking a quick nap," the manager said, "because he used to brag about how seamen learn to take quick naps at any time and in any place. But when I let myself into his apartment and poked him with my foot he didn't move. He was a real gentleman, and I'm certain his death could not possibly be attributed to any apartment-related injury." He looked satisfied. His job was done for the night.

I read the newspaper. Unable to watch late-night movies, with their endless stream of mindless, happy endings, I switched to mindless talk shows, to Letterman, or Leno, or anyone else who was content to sit around speaking to other people as if what they had to say mattered. One day I woke to find I had traced in crayon the outlines of the previous night's guests on the television screen. Without human flesh to fill them out, the lines looked like the skittering left by a needle measuring brain waves, or claw marks on the inside of a jar filled with yogurt.

I watched infomercials and sent away for the products they advertised: compilations of greatest hits, knives for cutting frozen food (why would I ever need to do that?), equipment to remove my midriff bulge, and stain-removing chemicals. The packages arrived and, as often as not, the next day I'd donate whatever it was I'd just bought to the Treasure Chest, where a woman named Ruth told me what a lovely person I was.

"I'm only trying to lend a hand," I would answer, "but you're welcome."

One night I was watching a news program when I heard the reporter say, "Dog breaks bank at Las Vegas, stay tuned." A commercial for tile cleaner came on. I went to the kitchen, and when I returned the reporter said that a few days earlier a dog, aided by a blind man, had entered a major casino. Apparently the animal, pretending to be a guide dog, had been spotted—too late—counting cards at a blackjack table, and nudging the blind man to tell him when to place his bets. The pair had gotten away with over four hundred thousand dollars. The surveillance tape showed a dog that was more black than brown, its ears hanging at the sides of its head like tiny hand towels, and on its face an expression of slightly bored, amused intellect. The blind man looked like a real blind man, but was shabby, as if he'd been hired only for the afternoon.

13

Something was happening with Gertrude; that was for sure. From time to time she dropped hints that big changes were under way, but when I asked if they involved me (I dared not say "the basement"), she was both cheery and infuriatingly vague. "You'll know as soon as I have something concrete to report" was all she'd say, and then she'd disappear again. She brought by a pie every once in a while, but nothing like the old days, and I noticed that sometimes she put in too much sugar or forgot to put in any sugar at all. Meanwhile, in the basement everything stayed the same: the chairs, the table, the stack of cardboard file boxes, and the dimly lit cylinders of the remaining women glowing in the gloom. The money was still coming, but it had dropped off still further since the loss of Rosita, maybe to half of what it used to be. The old guys had taken my measure and found me lacking.

Still, I did my job. Each night I walked around the dusty room, past the black woman, the blonde, the Asian woman, and Mary Katherine. I checked each cylinder for leaks and monitored its fluid level. I passed the base of what had been the Inuit woman's cylinder, where about an inch of viscous liquid still pooled at the bottom. On its surface a dead moth floated like a tiny, lost ice floe, and I felt a familiar sickening tightness in my chest. "I'm sorry," I found myself saying beneath my breath, then adding, not even sure what I meant by it, "I'll make it up to you."

When I had finished I went home to my apartment. Across the way from me, where the captain used to live, were a single mom and her kid, a noisy, skateboarding maniac. The grass and plants around the walkways were dying and no one seemed to care.

What was I waiting for? I knew I had to take action before it was too late. I *would* take action. I *would* bring those women back to life; but *how*, without losing another one? It was like staring into the innermost part of my soul and finding there, standing at the very bottom, only a tiny man holding out a cup of plain vanilla yogurt.

More out of desperation than anything else I found myself spending more time in Mister Twisty's basement, sleeping on a small cot I'd set up. Maybe I thought I would gain inspiration, or at least a clue, from the women themselves, but there too I was disappointed. Instead of dreams, all I had were more nightmares of the Soviet factory (*why* had I ever watched that stupid film?), with me inside a water boiler. And during the daytime, every Latina, or in fact any woman with dark hair who walked through the store's front door, would set my heart pounding as if Rosita, protected by those layers of foam, had somehow survived her bad night in the Dumpster, woken, and crawled out, barely the worse for wear. By then, of course, she would be really, really upset, and looking for the man she'd seen who had pointed to himself as she was drowning, grinning like the fool he was; and when she found him she would make him pay *con gusto*.

But if Rosita was out there, or for that matter the poor nameless Inuit, there was nothing I could do about it. On the surface, true, it seemed simple: just get the women out of their solution quickly. But if I did that, I would be back once again to the "plate-cracking effect." I went around and around and got nowhere. I slept, and then slept more. I missed the next Dumpster day, and another and another. The pies ceased completely, and Gertrude was at Mister Twisty's less than ever. When she did show up it was usually in the company of some man with a clipboard, and often with Matt, who took advantage of his visits to treat me as if we were old pals. Something was in the air, but what?

At last, one night following a meal of pepperoni pizza and an Orange Swirl, I had a dream in which Rosita, the Inuit, and I—all three of us—climbed out of the same water boiler (it had mysteriously gotten larger in my dream) and then climbed over a chain-link fence into a public swimming pool that had been closed due to high coliform bacteria levels. I used a crowbar to break the lock. Once inside, however, for some reason we swam only underwater, now and then coming up to breathe before resubmerging. That was all there was to it: no fellow swimmers, no lifeguard, no paddleboards, no towels tossed in careless bunches.

I awoke with a start. What did it mean, this swimming for a while underwater, then coming to the surface to catch a breath, and then diving back down again? The answer was obvious. "Listen to me, Jonathan," the dream was telling me. "All you have to do is place the next girl you choose to revive in a pool of water, and then add the detergent in the same way you did for poor Rosita. But this time, you ridiculous man, hold her head above the surface so she can breathe." It was so simple that I couldn't believe I hadn't thought of it on my own.

———————

But what kind of pool should I use? Clearly a public swimming pool, even if I could somehow manage to get one all to myself, would not be practical for such an undertaking. I needed a tank of some sort, one long enough for a reclining woman to stretch out comfortably while the solution of yogurt could be rinsed from her body, probably with a hose; and then, after she had been covered with regular water—this part of the process would last only a minute—the antibacterial stuff could be squirted into the tank in a smooth and steady motion as I held her head above the surface.

A bathtub would be too heavy to carry down to the basement by myself, so to use one I would have to take the woman back to my apartment, which was out of the question, of course. I thought about a vinyl wading pool, but suppose it sprang a leak in the middle of the process? I remembered just such a pool my mother had bought me when I was a child, and it lasted less than a day. I couldn't chance it. Fortunately

I remembered my last visit to Pets Incorporated, the day I'd purchased Steve Junior. Along the store's back wall had been a gigantic, empty fish tank. It was made—Steve had informed me in response to my question—"to hold very big fish."

It wouldn't be cheap, I knew, but how could anyone put a price on human life? Anyway, the twenty-percent discount would help; but even without a price break, in a way buying it would be a small, secret tribute to services rendered. It was Steve who had sold me his namesake, the rat who, like the first cosmonaut lost in space, had paved the way for others to follow. One day, if everything went well, I would construct a monument in the center of a public park in the shape of a gigantic human brain, and on top of that brain would be a small, friendly-looking Steve Junior, just sitting there. A plaque at the base would read "Good Friends."

"Fish, sure," Steve Senior remarked when I pointed out the tank. "I thought I sold you a rat a while back. What happened to him?"

Here was a guy, I noted for future use, who had an insufferably long memory. I would have to be careful.

"Pneumonia," I replied. "Anyway, Trudy is feeling a whole lot better these days, mostly thanks to all those pets you sold her. It's amazing how much they helped, but you know how women are. Now that she's feeling better she says she no longer needs them. But—if I can speak to you man to man, Steve—I'm afraid I'm here for myself this time. I've been going through a lot of emotional stress lately, and I thought I'd try out that pet business for myself. However, I'm not sure I can handle flesh and blood at this moment, so suppose I begin slowly, say with a really big fish tank. I'll throw in a few floating objects to see how I like them. And then, if they work out, I can come in later and buy lots of fish from you."

"Hmm," was Steve's reply, but he knocked down the price, sold me the tank, and even lifted one end to help me carry it over to Mister Twisty's. The thing was a lot heavier than I'd thought it would be.

"Where do you want it?" Steve asked, as we lurched through the front door of the yogurt parlor.

"I'll decide later," I told him. "For now, why don't we just lay it in front of the door to the basement, and when the time comes, I'll take care of it."

I gave Steve a complimentary cup of plain vanilla with toasted almonds on top. "Hey, by the way, now that Trudy's cheered up, do you suppose she's interested in giving you-know-who another try?" he asked.

"Well," I said, "soon, I think. But at the moment she seems to be a bit preoccupied."

Steve nodded, finished his yogurt, and went back to Pets Incorporated. For all the man's faults (smelling of pet shop, poor grooming, an overlong memory), he seemed to be patient, at least.

After he left, I sat at the counter and tried to figure out how I could get the heavy tank down the stairs and into the basement by myself. Glancing around the shop, I saw an apron hanging on a wall next to a chalkboard that announced Infinite Vanilla, a flavor that was exactly the same as what used to be regular vanilla, but the new name Gertrude had given it had doubled its sales. "Infinite Vanilla," I muttered under my breath. I got up from my stool and knotted together a half dozen aprons to form a circle. Then I looped one end around the far end of the fish tank. Twisting the loop once to make the symbol for infinity, I slipped the other end around my waist. Next I pushed the tank to the top of the basement stairs and balanced it carefully until one end hung off the top step, gave it a little shove and, bracing my feet so I wouldn't be dragged off balance and wind up spraining an ankle or breaking a leg, walked myself and the tank slowly down the steps until at last the far end of the tank rested on the basement floor. I stepped out of the loop and, taking care not to crack the glass, lowered my end to the ground. Finally I dragged the tank to the center of the room near the drain. After I collected several saltine wrappers the old men had not bothered to pick up, I looked around.

There the women all were, dozing in their solution, waiting to be awakened, and for once but really soon. I was ready to act, and my first thought was to jump right in and send Mary Katherine up to bat, until I thought about the past. Not so fast, Jonathan, I told myself. If you know anything, it's that things don't always go smoothly. I was ninety-five percent sure the tank thing would work, maybe even ninety-nine percent, but that missing percentage point still troubled me. Mary Katherine was temporarily out of the running, so would it be the black woman, the blonde, or the Asian? It was not easy to play God.

I flipped a coin. And then I flipped it again. It was the blonde.

Now all I had to do, if only to cover myself against the slim chance something might go wrong, was to wait a few more days, until just before they emptied the mall's Dumpsters.

I wasn't stupid.

14

Not surprisingly, with such important business ever closer at hand, filling a parade of cups and cones with frozen yogurt for one's basic spectrum of humanity seemed trivial, maybe even insulting. People walked in and complained about St. Nils's weather. They ordered a cone or a cup of one flavor or another. They took it away or they sat in the store and ate it. A couple of days later they were back telling me that the weather had changed. "No kidding," I told them, and meanwhile I tried to take a spiritual approach, to see in the humble act of repetition the necessary preparation that would make me worthy of the task that lay before me. I wasn't making much headway and business continued to be sparse. Then, two days before Dumpster Day, as I'd come to think of it, Bernie burst through the front door.

"The usual?" I asked as he dived straight behind the counter with a flashlight and his clipboard.

"Thanks," Bernie said. "I'd like that." He sounded troubled.

A couple of minutes later he emerged, and I set the cup of peach yogurt down in front of him. I'd been right. He *was* upset.

"Jonathan," he said, lowering his voice even though there were no customers in the shop, "there's a lot of pressure from downtown to produce results these days, so I'm going to say that you've just got to get that rat problem under control immediately. I don't know who, but somebody phoned in a tip that you have rats here, and as a matter of fact, I should write out a citation today. If headquarters learned that I let a big one like this go, I could lose my job. I haven't known you for all that long, but I can tell you're not a bad guy by the way you stepped up to bat after Spinner died, and Trudy deserves a break too—she's been through a lot recently. So I'm going to give you both another chance." I could see he was sweating.

He tapped the clipboard on the counter for emphasis and zipped up his windbreaker, which, after all, seemed a funny name to give a jacket. I should have been worried, but what struck me instead was how insignificant Bernie was just then, so full of his petty concerns about rodent droppings and the like, as he sat at the end of the counter, moving the wheatgrass to one side so he could scoop up the yogurt with his tiny white plastic spoon. Why did he ask for wheatgrass if he was not going to eat it? I couldn't help myself; I laughed under my breath. Beneath Bernie's feet, one of the major scientific breakthroughs of the century was about to take place, and yet he, poor dope, didn't have a clue.

"Is something funny?" he asked.

"Bernie," I said, "you have a few cobwebs stuck to your baseball cap that you may want to take care of."

He looked up at me, confused, then turned and said something about bringing a surprise by for me one of these days, but I was so busy thinking about bringing the blonde woman downstairs back to life that I missed his exact words.

"Sure," I said. "Anytime, Bernie. Whatever you say."

He started to add something, then apparently thought the better of it, because he just walked out the door, shaking his head and leaving a trail of wheatgrass along my newly swept floor; but for once I didn't care. I was still thinking about the blonde: What would she say to me? What would her first words be? Would she be shy? How would she express her gratitude?

Then the day before Dumpster Day arrived, and that night as I sat in the basement after the shop had closed, killing time by reading my file of yogurt recipes, I reflected how, from that moment forward, I might never have to worry again about something so trivial as pleasing customers whose palates had been jaded by having too many flavors to choose from in the first place. All this scheming about how to fill every minute of one's life with a series of never-ending pleasurable experiences—eating yogurt being only one example out of many— how trite it seemed compared to the power of life and death. First, I would revive the blonde, and next the Asian woman, and after her the black woman. When I was sure these first three had come through the reanimation process without harm, and only then, I would bring back Mary Katherine. Once they were all there, a foursome, they might even form a support group. I'd have to get rid of the old guys, of course, but how hard could that be? After far, far too long, fate was rearranging itself to be on my side again.

I checked my watch; it was time. Once again, I found myself unscrewing the cap of a cylinder. I set up the aluminum ladder alongside it, climbed, and lowered the same sling of aprons I had used to move the tank into the liquid, snagging the blonde's slippery bottom. I gave a tug and out she came, much lighter than I would have guessed—a relief because my back had been giving me problems ever since I'd had to lift Rosita out of her cylinder. Carrying the blonde over to the fish tank, which I had half filled with water, I laid her down carefully and hosed off the excess solution. Then, as my right hand held the hose to fill the rest the tank, with my left I held her head above the surface so she wouldn't drown.

When the tank was topped off I dropped the hose with a rubbery clunk, shut off the water, and hurriedly squirted in the Dawn. Everything was going exactly as I'd planned.

This time, maybe because of her relatively slender frame, there was an almost immediate reaction. The blonde woman was so thin that no sooner had I let loose the first squirt of the detergent than I could see her chest begin to throb. A pulse started in her neck, her pale skin flushed, and her hands began to rub her thighs in a light, quick motion, as if she'd been baking and had gotten a little flour on them. Her eyes remained shut, but her legs began to tremble, her feet curled forward, and her toes began to twitch. Then her knees bent, her arms shook, and she grasped the sides of the tank and pulled herself into a sitting position. What a privilege it was to be there at this second birth for her. Plus, I couldn't help but notice that in the flesh she was even more beautiful than she had been behind glass, so to speak.

The woman's limbs moved yet more rapidly, fluid dripped

from her pale hair, and her skin came alive in a uniform blush. Then all at once she made a tremendous heave and came unsteadily to her feet, splashing water out of the tank and onto my shoes and the floor. The next thing I knew she was shaking herself off, and then, with her eyes still shut tight, she began to flail her legs and arms wildly, like a bird attempting to take flight. She began to run furiously and madly away from me, narrowly missing the table in the center of the room, and straight into the far wall, where she slumped in a motionless heap.

Quickly I ran to her, jumping over a puddle, and felt for a pulse.

Nothing.

I turned her head, but her eyes stayed shut; she had never even looked at me.

What happened? I asked myself.

Then little by little, and far too late, I understood the facts of the matter: holding her head up out of the detergent mixture so that she might breathe, I had prevented her from drowning, but it was also possible that I had prevented her brain from reviving. Her body had come back, and magnificently, spurred by its autonomic nervous system, or maybe a burst of unused energy that had been left over from her previous existence before she had been placed in her cylinder. But that couldn't last for long, and it didn't. Like a decapitated chicken, this brave woman had moved, even run, but without a working brain the truth was that she never had a chance. And it had been completely my fault.

"I am so terribly, terribly sorry," I mouthed, taking care not to make a sound, so that I would not have to hear the pathos of those too, too empty words. I mopped up the water, hung the dripping sling over the ladder to dry, and then carried my burden, as light as she was, though only in a physical sense, to the alley behind Pets Incorporated. The walk to the Dumpster had never seemed so far. When we finally arrived, I laid a single strip of foam on top of her, tucking in the sides. I made sure the foam stayed in place by putting two discarded cans of cooking oil on top of it. The cans resembled nothing so much as birthday candles, half burnt, on top of a yellow cake from which someone had scraped every last piece of frosting. I shut the Dumpster's lid and walked back home.

15

So once again my hopes melted around me. Once again, any belief I'd allowed to take root that I could overcome the accidents of my past, any hint of pride that I—either through hard work or sheer luck—would ever have the skill to fix things that had been broken, to repair the damages of time, to dicker with the high cost of ignorance and circumstance, had slipped to zero—no, clear into the land of negative numbers. All the feeble plans I'd ever made for my success now returned to mock me. "How," they asked me, "could you ever have been so stupid? What," they inquired, "could you possibly have been thinking?"

And it was true that I had been discouraged—*very* discouraged—any number of times in my life; but after my last imbecilic effort to rescue the blonde woman, I must say that from that point on, even to get out of bed, to brush my teeth, to find a stick of deodorant, to lift my arms, and to rub it around in a patch of fuzzy armpit hair so as not to offend my customers became next to impossible. Even this last act, as simple as it might seem, was a much more hopeful statement about life than I could make at that moment. I walked with my arms mostly at my sides.

But paradoxically, at the same time, this total and complete hopelessness also had the effect of making things more clear. Granted, I was potentially in big trouble at that very moment, and one way or another I might have been indirectly responsible for the loss of life in others, but this wasn't going to be about blame. Things happened because they happened; everyone knew that. The real point was that I did not need to attract more customers to Mister Twisty's, or to be witty, or charming, or to become a good dancer or learn to play the piano or much of anything else at all. None of those were my job, and I could leave them to more talented souls. No, all I had to do was to figure out how to prevent the next woman from drowning. If I could do that one thing, and that one thing only, I would redeem myself. I'd be home. My job would be finished. I would be a success.

But did recognizing this make things easier? Of course not. As much as I hated to admit it, my track record looked bad, and had I been a betting man, I am not sure I would have backed myself. "You," I wanted to tell each unsuspecting customer who walked through the doors of Mister Twisty's, "you think you are looking at a contented employee of a comfortable suburban yogurt shop (and one who gets full health benefits, too, thanks to Gertrude), but you are wrong, wrong, wrong. Because the person you are looking at has been given only one thing to do, out of the countless things people can accomplish in life, and guess what? He can't even do that."

Still, I somehow dragged myself to work each day, and somehow I got through the infinity of days in every week, never checking even once on the women in the basement (I know, I know—I was supposed to keep the acidophilus going, but it was just too painful to go down there again). Somehow I came home, heated up the same frozen dinner, meatloaf with cheddar soup on top—though it wasn't actually the *same* dinner, but the same type of dinner—night after night. Now that I was mostly staying in my apartment, my old ways got the best of me: I turned on the TV, turned off my brain, and slept. Each day smeared into the next like a scoop of Raisin Rumba left out in the sun, and surely, when I think about it now, I know I *must* have gone *somewhere* to purchase those frozen dinners, but I just don't remember actually traveling to do it. I took no walks and, outside the confines of Mister Twisty's, I spoke to no one. I avoided Pets Incorporated and, in particular, Dumpsters.

There was a heat wave that might possibly have been a result of global warming, the television said, and so the pace of worldwide extinctions was picking up. Eventually, as with the numbers Alice's Bakery, a few doors down from Mister Twisty's, used to have its customers take, it would reach the human race itself, and maybe, it occurred to me, if it moved really quickly, I might get to be its spokesperson. If so, I was ready: "We were hopeless; we couldn't learn to act when it was needed; we couldn't save the smallest thing, let alone ourselves," I would say to the audience of roaches and maybe crustaceans out in the hall. Still, it's an ill wind that blows no good. As a result of global warming, business at Mister Twisty's had improved, and those few times I saw her, Gertrude seemed even more cheerful, at times almost manic. "Life is change, Jonathan," she told me once in passing, and I have to say that made me worry more than anything.

Then one night, while I was lying on the couch, exhausted from the day's work, my head propped on my arms, my body wrapped in a thin blanket, somewhere between waking and sleep, I had another dream. But it wasn't, thank God, about those horrible boilers again, nor was it at the swimming pool. Rather it was a vision in which I was standing outdoors staring at an enormous elm, the leaves of which were healthy and green, except where a cylinder of a squirrel's scruffy nest poked out. On the main trunk was a hole through which honeybees entered and left—the entrance to a hive, evidently—though I was unable to tell if the bees were threatening or only going about their business.

It was, as always in my dreams, a temperate day. As I allowed my body to relax into this scene of rustic beauty, I saw that a river was flowing by directly in front of me, just past the elm. It was not a huge river, but one of medium width, with a nearby waterfall, stage left, that was only about six feet from top to bottom, an ordinary waterfall. It wasn't the kind anyone would ever bother to put on a postcard, but to me it was even more beautiful for its modesty. It occurred to me that if the bees attacked for some reason, I could dive into the river and it would keep me safe. For the first time in a long time, I felt a wonderful wave of peace wash over my body.

Then I lifted my gaze and saw that on the opposite bank of the river, maybe thirty-five feet away, was a man who looked uncannily like Captain Bloxheim, dressed as he had been the last time I saw him. He wore a bathrobe and pajamas and a peaked naval hat, and he was spraying the water from his hose straight into the river. His skin was still ashen, and he looked weak, but the palm tree tattooed on his arm had been restored to its former state of health. Now he was shouting something at me that I couldn't make out over the roar of the water, and he was pointing.

I looked upriver, in the direction he indicated, hoping to find a clue as to the content of his message. Above me, all I saw was a graceful canopy of trees of the usual sort. I stared out at the rapidly moving surface of the water. Perhaps, I thought, he was telling me to watch out for something of interest floating downstream, but there was nothing but a carpet of debris: torn pieces of fallen leaves, dead insects and living ones, minnows, thistles, chips of wood, twigs, logs, and straw, all going over the edge together, like Elberta, like the captain, like that Cub Scout and the old lady, like Spinner, like Sparkles, Steve Junior, the mice, my father, the Inuit woman, the blonde, Rosita, and, yes, like me.

"What are you trying to say?" I shouted across the river to him. "Is there some kind of answer you are trying to give me? Can't you speak up a little? Try."

I looked at the captain again and attempted to decipher the exact content of his message from the movement of his lips. All I could make out was just one word of two syllables repeated over and over, and that word seemed to be, although I could not be absolutely sure, "Good-bye."

I could feel a flood of tears rising behind my eyes, and then everything went white, as if I had become one of those dozens and dozens of pieces of straw that were passing over the waterfall at that minute, plunging straight into the realm of froth and air, of light without body, a mind without consciousness, a migraine without the pain— was that even possible? I thought a migraine *was* pain—a revelation without content.

Here there was no loss, or happiness either, nothing but light, sometimes a wave but at other times a particle, though there was no one around to care; no one was thinking "particle" or "wave"; no one was thinking at all. It was only energy, only potential, only Being, and what was to be done with this Being wasn't important, just its potential. Then I awoke.

"Good-bye," was what the vision had told me.

The very next day, I was at Mister Twisty's holding my hands over my ears (how the sound of those trash trucks bothered me!), when a familiar face came into view. The face was familiar because it belonged to a man I had just served a Blueberry Swirl a couple of minutes earlier, and now that same face was red with anger. I signaled as best I could (while still keeping my hands over my ears) that if the man to whom the face belonged would remain patient for a few extra moments until the trucks had passed I would be happy to answer his question, if indeed a question was what he had. When I finally removed my hands from my ears, he began to shout.

"What is wrong with you anyway? I've been asking for a straw for the past two minutes, and the whole time you've just been standing there like one of those blind, deaf, and dumb monkeys. I don't know what your story is, buddy, but how am I supposed to drink this without a straw?"

I stared at him while his words resonated in my ears as in one of those old movies where, through the use of an echo chamber, the director is able to indicate a character's deepest thoughts: "without a straw . . . a straw . . . a straw . . ."

Yes! That was it! I would give the next woman a straw to breathe through while her head remained underwater.

I had six whole days left before the Dumpster was to be emptied again behind Pets Incorporated.

And if the preceding time, however long it had been, had moved slowly, the time that followed that revelation suddenly accelerated, fishtailing down the track—the same track, I suppose, that must have been repaired after the car of my mind lost control the first time I saw Mary Katherine down in the basement of Mister Twisty's after all those years, with a burst of smoke from its screeching tires. The hot weather persisted, but at least I was back to being able to tell one day from the next. Meanwhile, I hurried about shopping for straws and testing them: from the traditional sort, to the flexible ones, to the extra-thick variety intended for malts and the like, the kind of straw I refused to use at Mister Twisty's because the thin ones, even used two at a time, made customers' drinks last longer so that they thought they were getting more. In the end, I decided that it was the principle of the straw that was important, not the straw itself, and so I walked down to McReedy's Hardware to buy a section of one-inch PVC pipe. I got a three-foot length, long enough to be sure an end wouldn't accidentally become submerged. That and a roll of duct tape.

"You ready for another case of that cleaner yet?" McReedy asked as I stood fidgeting at the counter. He looked the same as always, large and nosy, with puffy skin and an unhealthy pallor.

"Soon," I said. "Right now I seem to have a minor plumbing problem, which is why I need this pipe and this tape. It's nothing serious."

"And your rats? How are they doing?"

"Oh," I said, "rats . . . Actually I don't have any; I never did. It's just because . . . I told you . . . I heard that some of the other places in the mall have been having a little problem."

"That's right, I remember now," McReedy said slyly. "By the way, I think you'll be interested in a little idea I have for the next mall meeting. It's about us all hiring a new trash company. I found one that's cheaper, uses much smaller containers, and comes twice a week. I hear it lowers the rodent problem significantly." He looked at me and winked.

I told him I'd think about it. Walking back to Mister Twisty's, I spotted a dead rat next to the entrance of Buffalo Bill's Chicken Wings, a new addition to our mall. It was not Steve Junior.

I returned to the yogurt parlor and carried the stuff down to the basement. It was the first time I had been down there in a while, and I was sorry to see that it was looking shabbier than ever and more forlorn, like a distant memory. True, the three women who remained looked healthy enough—I took care to throw in some fresh yogurt starter—but now two out of the original six cylinders simply stood vacant, half full of whatever fluid remained. The other cylinder, the one I'd pulled off its base while trying to rescue the Inuit woman, still lay in its corner. The last of her liquid had finally evaporated, leaving only a layer of whitish powder that looked like snow. The table was there, and of course the chairs, but the money had dropped off considerably. I picked up what was there, but clearly, with three women out of commission, the old guys seemed to think they could leave behind whatever they felt like. On the one hand, I thought, I should confront them, but on the other, why bother? Soon, very soon in fact, they would have no reason at all to come to Mister Twisty's.

Back upstairs, when I opened the shop again, I found that there was an unexplainable run on Mint Magic yogurt, and then, as so often happens in the yogurt business, the run switched to plain chocolate. Then, as if the chocolate had been a sort of warning buzzer, it switched to no business at all. So the place was empty when Gertrude walked in, alone for once, her skin glowing as if she'd just gotten a facial a few doors down at Pretty Face.

"Jonathan," she said excitedly, "it's settled, so I can tell you." She signaled that I should come around the counter and join her at the stools.

I didn't like the sound of it, but Gertrude didn't seem to notice. "I'm sorry to have been preoccupied of late, but although you and I have done some great things with Mister Twisty's, I'm sure it hasn't escaped you that I've been bringing a lot of people by to look around of late."

I made a sound that I hoped would indicate that, yes, I had noticed it, but that Matt and I would never be friends.

Gertrude picked up a napkin and folded it into a triangle. "But maybe I should begin at the beginning. You were there, of course, when Claude died, and you know how upset I was back then." She looked at me, and for a moment, despite all the grief-management work she had done recently, I could see the effects of Spinner's death ripple across her face.

"I don't know how I would ever have made it without Spouses Without Spouses—and you, naturally—but then, after I had been in the group awhile I realized that support is only one part of overcoming a significant loss. Another part, and maybe more important than any of the others, is to move on and accept new challenges that are significantly different from the ones we are familiar with."

Gertrude smiled brightly and twisted the napkin into a sort of rabbit-eared piece of napkin-sculpture. Then she recovered her composure and resumed. "So I started to think to myself: I have this brand that already has considerable power in the marketplace, even if it has slipped a little of late. How can I take that and parlay it into something newer? What can I do that would be more in the spirit of the here and now, as Mister Twisty's used to be back when Claude started it? What can I do that might be more of a cutting-edge experience, tied into, say, something in the arts?"

I told her I'd have to think about it.

"Actually," she continued, "you don't have to. You'll be pleased that, with a little help from Matt, I've come up with an idea all my own. And what I've been thinking is that I could turn Mister Twisty's into a small restaurant—nothing complicated, maybe just soup and a salad bar—but after that takes off, then in the basement I could have a jazz club, one that serves natural foods. Suppose we took away those awful ski poles from Mister Twisty and stuck a trumpet in his hand? Wouldn't that send a terrific message to the community about what we stand for? We could even keep the name."

All I could do was gulp.

"And, Jonathan, you do enjoy poetry, don't you? Because I was thinking that on weeknights we could have poetry readings to attract diners. Matt has a lot of contacts in the world of jazz and the like, Jonathan, and I'm thinking this could be a real contribution to the arts, if you know what I mean. How does that sound to you?"

I told her it sounded fine.

"Well," she said, "if you are interested I'll give you this CD you can listen to. It's by Matt's cousin. He plays the saxophone and is looking to start a combo. I don't suppose you play an instrument, do you?" I shook my head and she gave me a small hug. "And now I've got a lot of things to do," Gertrude concluded. Then she left.

The time for waiting was over. Any day now Gertrude would go down to the basement, and although I could surely invent some explanation for empty cylinders, if the women were still in them I would be in trouble. The trash men would not come to empty the Dumpsters for a few more days, but I had made my mind up—I no longer needed to wait for them. This time there would be no need for a Dumpster. This time it was now or never. This time I could not possibly fail, and for once I knew without question who would be next. This time I would act.

I took Matt's cousin's CD and tossed it in the wastebasket.

16

That night, as I descended the stairs, each step creaked out its own alternative prophecy of my future, some in cheerful squeaks, others in low groans (which I dismissed), accompanied, as in the soundtrack to some slow-motion dream, by the crunch of grit beneath the sturdy soles of my shoes. Once again I watched as the basement's single incandescent bulb—through the elementary optical illusion created by my going down the steps—appeared to drop in stages from the ceiling. I had already noted the basement's gray cinder-block walls and gray concrete floor a hundred times, but this time, near several of the walls, I spotted surprisingly large balls of dust, some more than six inches in diameter—dust bunnies, I think they're called—even as the cylinders themselves, formerly the vessels of so much of my speculation and hope even that very morning, seemed now only crude and heavy, their glowing liquid gloomy, their glass walls smudged and streaked with grease and fingerprints, the detritus of someone else's nightmares. There was no trace of the old guys at all, not even any money. Had they sensed something was up and abandoned me before I could abandon them?

If I had been more media-savvy, I realized too late, I might have rented a video camera from Ed's Discount Electronics a few doors down and recorded the whole event for posterity; but instead I would have to content myself with the pixels of my own memory. Soon I would have the answer to the mystery of Mary Katherine, and then, good news or bad, I would release the others back into the world as quickly as I could. Gertrude's new plans meant that I would have to give up the idea of a slow reentry—maybe instead drop off all three remaining women at a mental health clinic or a singles bar. In any case, they would be free, and so would I.

Around me stood Mary Katherine, the Asian, and the black woman, like solemn judges in a court of last resort. I took the length of white plastic pipe from where it had been leaning against the wall. There were a few rat droppings next to it, but the pipe itself was clean. Then I tore off several strips of duct tape and stuck them lightly on one side of Mary Katherine's tank, where I could reach them easily. Once the critical resuscitation process had begun, I wanted no wasted motions. "Soon," I told the woman who bore such an uncanny resemblance to my ex-girlfriend. "Soon."

I looked at the woman I called Mary Katherine as she was then for the last time: dormant and mysterious, a perfect crystal of silence about to be shattered. She was a Sleeping Beauty, a Snow White, whoever, trembling on the brink of being brought magically back to life by means of an ordinary household-cleaning product. Her auburn hair floated like those plates around the heads of medieval saints; her skin was as smooth and perfect as a Renaissance Madonna's; her breasts were voluptuous and chaste; the delicate swirl of her navel was enigmatic. Soon this picture would begin to move. She would speak; she would have questions, opinions. She would probably need some exercise after having been cooped up all that time. She would become emotional. She might tell me about the Sorbonne and ask about the number of species that had become extinct since she first entered her long sleep. Or, I had to admit, more probably, if she *were* a complete stranger, she would be carrying to me a whole new story, one that was hers and hers alone, except for a small footnote following a number at the bottom of one of its pages: "Returned to life by Jonathan." Followed by a date.

Once again, I climbed the ladder and carefully unscrewed the lid of the cylinder. This particular lid, for whatever reason, was a bit tougher to turn than the rest. Did that mean she'd been there longer than the others? Maybe she would be able to tell me, and after that I could enlist her help in explaining the whole situation to the other two women after we revived them together.

I took the same apron sling I'd used earlier and slid it carefully under Mary Katherine's unresisting buttocks. I lifted. This was the moment that would justify and pardon everything else in my life that had come before. *Everything.*

I shifted Mary Katherine's dripping body onto my shoulders and hurriedly staggered to the waiting fish tank, leaving behind a thick trail of slime across the basement floor and on me as well. Carefully, I laid her down inside the tank and inserted the breathing pipe between her lips, sealing it around her mouth and nose with the duct tape, which I secured behind her head so that there would be no leaks. She still slept on, just as she had one afternoon back in college when she had failed to awaken after a little morning lovemaking and slept though a midterm exam in invertebrate zoology, nearly failing the course as a result. Then I secured her hands with the duct tape so she wouldn't be able to pull the pipe out of her mouth. I reached for the hose, turned it on, and began to cover her with water.

"Any minute now, whoever-you-are," I told her, and my heart pounded so violently from the exertion of carrying her and the sheer excitement of the moment that it seemed as if I could hear it outside my body, pounding away with heavy, dull, shuddering thuds. I placed my free hand on her lips and pressed the duct tape tight to be sure it didn't leak. Everything was going perfectly.

And then the pounding *was* outside my body. Someone was banging on the actual door to the basement, the door that, fortunately, I had locked behind me. I looked for the bottle of Dawn, which I seemed to have misplaced. But before I could find it, unbelievably, the door crashed open, and the pounding became a whole herd of heavy feet crashing down the wooden stairs. The first pair belonged to Bernie, who held a flashlight in one hand and his clipboard in the other. The second pair, slower and more hesitant, belonged to Gertrude; the third, fourth, fifth, sixth, and seventh belonged to people whom I recognized as members of the Spouses Without Spouses crowd, including Mister Fix-It himself, Matt, all of them wearing those strange yellow shirts with bees on them.

"Jonathan," Bernie said, "what the . . . ?"

For a second I could imagine the whole scene as it must have appeared to Bernie and the others: the glowing ring of cylinders, a woman lying in a fish tank, the trail of slime, the hose, the length of PVC, the strips of duct tape over her mouth and binding her wrists.

"Holy smoke!" Bernie and the rest of them must have thought.

But as for me, I'm proud to say instead of panicking, as others might have done, I felt an almost unnatural power seep into my flesh. This was *my* show at last, I told myself, and I'd waited a long time, much too long, to finally get it on the road.

I took a deep breath and raised my hand to call for calm. "Excuse me, everyone, please, will you please be patient for a few more minutes?" I asked. "This is a critical part of this procedure. I only need to complete one or two more details, and then, Bernie, and the rest of you, when I'm finished, I'll be happy to explain everything about this whole, and what must seem to you quite puzzling, business." I thought I sounded both very lucid and in control.

And whether Bernie *would* have sat down and listened to reason or not, I'll never know, because at that very moment, Gertrude opened her mouth. "Jonathan," she said, "what have you done?" Then she let out a giant groan, maybe from excitement, but it was a groan I knew only too well, having heard it from my own father's mouth, and next she dropped down heavily, her hand reaching for something out in front of her. "I'm cold," she said.

I watched a dime from Gertrude's purse roll slowly across the floor and come to a halt against the base of the Inuit's cylinder.

Was it the sight of Gertrude's collapse or his sense of responsibility as a servant of the public trust that set off some primitive reaction in Bernie? I don't know, but at that point he must have panicked, because he dropped the flashlight and clipboard, pulled out a small pistol from a back pocket, and pointed it at me (who would have guessed that the city allowed restaurant inspectors to carry personal firearms?). "You move over here right now, Jonathan," Bernie yelled, rather more forcefully than necessary, indicating, with his free hand, a spot about a dozen feet away from where I was standing. "You . . . you stay away from her! There will be plenty of time for explanations later."

"But . . . but . . ." I started to say, but Bernie waved the pistol again in a vicious fashion and looked as if he were about to explode.

"I'm cold," Gertrude repeated.

What choice did I have? I moved to where Bernie indicated and watched in horror as he, using only one hand, expertly dialed his cell phone. With the other he held the gun on me—all the more maddening as I was forced to stand helplessly and watch Mary Katherine's once-vibrant flesh grow flat and dull and stiff and gray. "Please," I said, but no one listened. She was dying before my eyes, and it was not the slightest compensation that, for once at least, it was somebody else's fault.

Time stopped, and for a while I knew how those women must have felt all those months they were inside their cylinders. When it began again, the paramedics, who must have been the recipients of Bernie's frantic call, arrived in a bunch and split their fruitless CPRs on Mary Katherine and poor Gertrude. Moments later the police, who in their turn must have been summoned by the paramedics, stormed down the stairs, gaped at the scene and, taking their cue from the Spouses Without Spouses, who were pointing to me as the person responsible for this situation, drew their own guns, threw me against a wall, searched me, and handcuffed me to a pipe.

And then, as Mary Katherine lay there already irretrievably dead, Mister Know-It-All, Matt, without asking me anything at all, stupidly unplugged the electric cords to the remaining two cylinders as if he were going to be a hero by preventing a further crime. So I watched as their lights went out and I heard the gentle muffled thudding of what must have been two pairs of knees and elbows, freed from whatever magnetic or other kind of force had been holding them in place, blindly bumping downward against the sides of the cylinder like the limbs of two dolls, like two twin bathyspheres heading toward the bottom of some black and unmeasurable ocean fissure.

"You fool! For God's sake," I begged, "hurry, just plug them back in. There's still time to save them!"

"You fucking monster," a tall police sergeant said. "Why should we listen to the likes of you?" I caught a glimpse of his nightstick raised over my head, and then everything, or at least my mind, went black.

And it was only when I woke again, still in handcuffs, my wrists nearly numb, that I had the chance to puzzle out what had happened, something you yourself no doubt already have deduced: namely that Bernie, driving home from a movie and seeing the lights on in Mister Twisty's—I must have forgotten to turn them off in my excitement—and thinking (correctly, as it turned out) that I was still on the premises, had decided to stop by for a surprise inspection (so *that* was the surprise he'd mentioned). Then, finding the door locked, he had been just about to leave when who should show up but Gertrude, whose idea it must have been, following their regular meeting, to give a few members of Spouses Without Spouses a quick tour of what was supposed to be her future restaurant/ jazz club. So it would have been Gertrude who let Bernie in with her key.

The rest, as you probably know, was in the newspapers.

17

Reflecting on the events of my life that followed that memorable evening, I suppose things went about the only way they could. After that first fierce round of clubbing by the overzealous officer—probably due as much to his adrenaline levels as anything—I was treated reasonably well, particularly when you consider that to all appearances I must have seemed to the police like some sort of deranged pervert of the worst possible sort. I tried to explain about the old guys but, needless to say, they had made themselves scarce, and if anyone believed me, they really didn't care. Why should they? The authorities had their monster. Still, I have to say that the police themselves, after things settled down, turned out to be a mostly decent group of guys, caught up in their own simplistic world of Right and Wrong, true, but mostly showing a fair amount of self-control and offering an occasional kindness.

Even so, for a long while, when I was really feeling down about myself, sometimes it seemed as if their low opinion of me might well have been correct. Maybe I *was* a monster, I thought to myself. Do monsters know that they are monsters?

And so this whole business was starting to get me down, until one morning—it was a Saturday—I woke and took stock. I asked myself: What had I really done? Was it really all my fault? I doubted it, any more than a person can take complete credit for any good they happen to do. And if I *was* guilty of something, when exactly did this so-called criminal behavior begin?

And say, just for argument's sake, that I *could* come up with a specific time when and place where everything, as they say, "started," what could I personally have done to make things turn out differently? Would the moment to prevent all of this have been even before the animal shelter episode—back, for example, in Mexico? Would it have made the least bit of difference if I'd tossed the stranger out of Carl's bus? Should I have decided to stay awake an extra few hours studying for my biology exam instead of writing the names of several phyla on the bottom of the brim of my baseball cap and being expelled from State College? Would taking a job at a pastry shop or an abattoir have really been better than one at a yogurt shop? Even if I had chosen correctly in each of these situations, if I had never eaten a bite of yogurt in my entire life, would anything I did or did not do have prevented those women from bobbing quietly in their jars? I doubt it.

So considering everything, I can't complain.

Because, as Bruce, my public defender, explained to me when the time for my trial rolled around, while on the one hand the incident at the animal shelter technically was inadmissible to this latest charge, on the other hand, the situation with the women in the basement seemed to have plenty going for it on its own.

Given public opinion, which was particularly inflamed at that point, we decided to skip the whole trial-by-jury business and go straight for the judge. We had chosen the Good Samaritan defense, and for about two hours I actually believed that Bruce and I were making headway along those lines, but then the thing that tipped it in the end was the testimony of Matt, who told the court that Gertrude had always said there was something strange about the way I acted, and that she'd told him before she died that she was about to fire me.

Needless to say, Gertrude wasn't around to argue.

So, in the end, I was condemned to death by lethal injection, which means, according to Bruce, who every month or so sends me a postcard telling me he's still working on my case, that I might have as long as twenty years to go, what with appeals and all, before I myself become extinct. Judging by the postcards, Bruce has been doing a lot of traveling, and he tells me he likes the weather in the Northwest. The rain doesn't bother him in the least, he says. I assume that he means well; and yet, I ask myself, what is extinction, anyway? Angels never existed, let alone became extinct, and they're still around, maybe even more of them than ever, in their fashion. I mean, if you asked anyone practically anywhere in the world to draw an angel, I'll bet that they could, just as every day you hear some unfortunate person or another being called a dodo. In other words, if you wanted to, you could probably draw me.

You could draw me, for example, right now, as I lie on my back in my simple bed, staring at the ceiling. My cell, by the way, is surprisingly comfortable—a quiet corner location that gets a bright and cheery chink of sun early every morning. Closer to the bars is a straight-backed chair made of light-colored pine, along with a small, light-gray metal desk, its surface supporting a yellow legal pad, and to my right is a metal cup that holds four stubby green pencils, only one of which has anything like an eraser to its name. On one wall I have my new prison-issued calendar, the next twelve months, with the important dates for my hearings circled in red. I have a chessboard, though no one seems much interested in getting up a game. All of this is standard stuff, of course, but in my case there's also a miniature refrigerator, sent by an anonymous donor, that's similar to the one I bought some time ago at the Treasure Chest for the basement. I keep fresh milk in it, and cartons of low-fat yogurt (everything you've heard about the tendency of prison food to pack on the pounds is only too true). The fridge is a pale blue, if that's important.

And, yes, I'm aware that it's more than the women had.

Sometimes I attend meetings of the Criminal Republicans for Jesus. They're a lively group of guys and have a stock-market investment fund that's doing pretty well these days. I think Gertrude would have admired their supportive atmosphere, except for the Jesus part.

I also have a small CD player and a few easy-listening CDs brought to me by Bruce on one of his rare visits. I think he feels bad for losing my case. The CD player is turned off right now because I kind of enjoy the sound of my fellow inmates yelling their complaints about the breakfast we've just finished (powdered eggs, freeze-dried potatoes, and watery coffee). It's the same breakfast we get every day, and yet it's heartening to hear how my peers can find new ways to be out-raged all over again each time it arrives. I guess they just don't give up, these criminals.

I have, though. "Forget those silly appeals," I told Bruce a couple of months ago when he showed up wearing a Hawaiian shirt and Bermuda shorts. "Can't we just accept things as they are?" But Bruce, who I think has watched too many lawyer shows, answered that it's his job to fight for justice, even in the most obviously reprehensible cases.

"I'm not talking about you, Jonathan," he said. "As an individual you're unimportant to me, because I'm fighting here for a principle, and for the rights of all those others who may follow in your sick criminal footsteps."

And speaking of lost causes, I've also given up trying to find out the identity of the woman I was just about to revive—Mary Katherine, or whoever. DNA, RNA—they all came up blanks; and anyway, to know for sure, to give her, or any of the women, her true name, would only make matters worse in the feeling-bad department. No matter who she was, she is equally dead by now, alas.

So through the mix of my fellow prisoners' voices, still grumbling, yelling insults back and forth and at the guards, I can hear the flushing of the pipes, the rattle of the bars, and also the quiet click of toenails on cement, the sound made by the prison's fierce police dogs as they patrol its perimeter all day to be sure that no one escapes.

Except that, come to think of it, one usually doesn't hear that particular quiet click of nails very often indoors, or at this time in the morning.

The clicking stops.

Now I can just barely make out the sound of someone inserting something—a key or a slender piece of metal—into my cell's lock and turning it.

I look up from where I was lying on my bed, startled, and, to my surprise, the cell door swings open, and I'm staring at a dog, a magnificent beast who looks to be part German shepherd, part rottweiler, part pit bull, and part chow. In his mouth he is carrying a sturdy canvas satchel, the kind that plumbers use.

"Buck?" I whisper.

He nods his huge head once and steps toward me.

"But how did you . . . ?" I'm about to ask, and then I remember all those articles in the paper, back when I'd tried to free him. I'd always wondered if he'd gotten around to reading them. If he had, he would, of course, have understood that I arrived at the shelter that day only trying to help. Then, following my trial (in what came to be called the Mister Twisty's case), there had been a second wave of articles in the tabloid press accusing me of all manner of crimes, plus a lot of television coverage as well. Buck must have put the two together, I think, and now he's arrived in person.

Buck pants, and as I give him a scratch beneath his chin, I can feel his moist, warm breath along my palm. He's a little gray around his muzzle, but his coat is glossy, his tongue is a healthy pink, his eyes are deep and dark, and all in all he looks better than the blackjack video.

I open the satchel. Inside is the complete uniform of a prison guard, neatly folded. It appears to be exactly my size.

"You tried to help me out when you thought I was in a jam, Jonathan." (Buck can't talk, of course, but he must be thinking this.) "Now it's my turn to do a good deed for you. Hurry up; take this guard uniform that I've hastily assembled. I'm sorry, but I had to guess your size from the photos in the newspaper, and I hope I got it right. See, here's a gray shirt, a pair of gray slacks, a gray tie, and black shiny shoes. You must put them on as quickly as possible so we can make our escape in a truck that I have arranged to be waiting near the gate. And oh, Jonathan, though I may be smart, I'm afraid you will have to drive."

And it isn't that I'm so overcome by gratitude that I don't sink to my knees and give the big dog a hug right then and there—I do—but then, even as I'm doing it, I think, Wait a minute, Buck. Where would we go, you and I? What would we do? Even with what must be a substantial bank account, the two of us, one a dog and the other a man, would both be fugitives.

I hear a low sound from Buck's throat, and stand up to see him motioning with his head toward the corridor. Time is running out, he is saying. He has calculated this escape of ours down to the minute, planning around the schedule of the guards. If I don't get moving, any minute now Fritz, the guard who's on duty this morning and who's actually not a bad guy, will find the two of us, and there'll be big trouble. Buck doesn't need to tell me; I know he's right.

Now Buck's taken my hand into his mouth, and I can feel the slight pressure of his teeth as he bites down softly. "It's urgent, Jonathan," is his unmistakable message. "Now or never."

But really, I think, what will happen to me if I leave?

Here I have the clang of bars, the really bad food, and the occasionally brutal guards, although it's hard to blame them because it must be crappy working here. Out there, what would there be? An endless chain of convenience store entrées? Another rented room? Another low-paying job? True, once outside I would have the chance to start a new life, but who could guarantee that it would turn out to be any better than this present one?

It's not more than a minute that I'm thinking this, but it feels like at least an hour.

I look long into Buck's dark, still eyes.

"No, Buck," I say. "Not today, or any day for that matter. Believe me, I can appreciate the immense effort it must have taken for you to orchestrate this whole scenario, and I'm certainly grateful. You can consider your debt to me, if there ever was one, paid in full. I'll talk to my attorney, and if I can, I'll even be happy to reimburse you for the cost of the uniform and the getaway-truck rental if you like, but I'm not going."

Buck looks at me, and then around, taking the whole place in—my cell, the corridor, and the other cells—as if for the first time. He nods to me once slowly to indicate that he understands, and then with his mouth picks up the bundle of clothing and returns it to the satchel. He closes it, using the leather thong attached to the zipper to pull it shut. Then he lifts it up and, locking my cell door behind him, walks over to the cell across from mine. It belongs to Malone, who's been here on death row for years as a result of selling contaminated vaccines to children. He's been leaning against his bars and watching this whole operation with increasing interest.

Buck opens the man's cell and drops the satchel at Malone's feet. Malone, I guess, still believes in what he might call "fresh starts," as do all the other guys like him, who never seem to learn, or get enough. Malone, I think, in whom hope springs eternal. I watch him bend over as he quickly dons the guard's uniform. It's a little small—particularly the shirt—for Malone, who spends hours every day pumping iron, but it will do.

The dog gives me one more look, as if to say, "Jonathan, you idiot, this was your last chance."

"Buck," I answer, "I know you're smart, but let's face it, you're only a dog, and although I can't speak directly to your experience, I *can* tell you that although species may come and go (some, unfortunately, forever), the sum of my own consciousness consists entirely of that pathetic series of events, that string of coincidental happenings I call my past. It's not much to be proud of, but whose life is? So bright or dim, good or bad, if it's to have any meaning at all, I can't just give it up. I had my time for action and now it's over. I'm sorry, big guy, but right now you're barking up the wrong tree. I have to stay with what I have."

Buck gives me one final look, and Malone throws in an embarrassed wave good-bye. In a day or two they'll bring someone else in to take his place, and Malone, when he's eventually caught again, because a guy like him always is, will wind up in a place even harder to escape from.

In other words, I do my time.

I wait for Bruce with his stacks of forms to fill out and his petitions and his strange taste in CDs.

In my dreams I see Mary Katherine, and Gertrude, the blonde, and Rosita, and the Inuit—all the women and me too, because I am there with them, wherever *there* is—and you are on the outside, looking in. Then, sooner or later, you will leave. You will leave, and if the day is warm you may find yourself inside a yogurt store, trying to choose a flavor right for you; I hope you find one that makes you happy. But in the meanwhile, remember all of us still locked away in prisons, and by memory, and by the chains of circumstance.

Remember me.

End

Writing this book would not have been possible without the help of many people. I'd like especially to thank first and foremost Lee Montgomery, and next Zach Braun, Dylan Landis, Mary Otis, John O'Brien, Martin Riker, Janice Shapiro, Meg Storey, and Monona Wali for their insightful readings and wise suggestions. A special thanks to Sue Taylor for her timely help with the cover illustration, and Myron Kunin and Taylor Acosta of Curtis Galleries for their generosity in making it possible. As always, of course, I am grateful to Jenny, my wife.